I0603217

THE LOST TREASURE OF THE JAMAICAN PIRATE

THE THIRD CHAPTER OF *THE LOST EL DORADO* SERIES

W. MICHAEL GAZDAR, DC

© 2021. All rights reserved.

W. MICHAEL GAZDAR, D.C.
Walnut Creek, California

Published and distributed by: John Muir Chiropractic Center (JMCC)
First Edition: 2021

2021 Ygnacio Valley Road, Suite C-204
Walnut Creek, California 94598
Phone: (925) 939-2225
Fax: (925) 939-8017

Email: michael@gazdar.com
Web: www.michaelgazdar.com

This book is a work of fiction. Names, characters, places and incidents are products of the author's imagination, and are used factitiously. Any resemblance to actual events, local people or persons living or dead is entirely coincidental.

No part of this book may be reproduced without the author's written permission.

Library of Congress Catalogue Number: 2021907900
Gazdar, Michael

THE LOST TREASURE OF THE JAMAICAN PIRATE

ISBN (e book): 978-0-9645301-5-7

ISBN (Trade Paperback): 978-0-9645301-4-0

Printed in the United States of America

ACKNOWLEDGEMENTS

Thank you to the following people who have helped make this book
a reality:

Cover Design by: Nicole Hayley Art

Publishing Assistance: Eric Van Der Hope

Back Cover Photo by: CBJ Gazdar

Formatting by: Nicole Hayley Art

Beta Readers: Janet Baillie
Captain Paul Ruff
Marilyn Hubbard

DEDICATION

This book is dedicated to my wife, Teri and our three sons, Christian,
Brandon and Jonathan.

You guys are my family, my loves and my life. Thank you.

CONTENTS

PROLOGUE

"DAMNATION SEIZE MY SOUL IF I GIVE YOU
QUARTERS, OR TAKE ANY FROM YOU."
BLACKBEARD THE PIRATE, (EDWARD TEACH)

THE JAMAICAN PIRATE WAS NOT USED TO taking prisoners. He looked out over the deck of his warship. In this case, a 70-foot-long fast boat that had once been used by the U.S. Navy in World War II, for sea rescues of pilots who had been shot down and other blue water duties. It was outfitted with four four-pound guns, both fore and aft, and also two single barrel .50 caliber machine guns on the sides. It was painted slate gray and flew no flags of country origin. He had obtained a smoke screen unit, used in WWII on PT boats as a getaway means of camouflage, when under attack by an enemy with superior strength. He was sure his boat was the most fearsome attack boat in these waters.

He had been doing this since he was 16. Working on gun ships, taking prisoners if necessary, working for a lot of bad people, some of whom wound up dead of course, due to their stupidity, but he, nonetheless, was good at his trade. At over 6'5" tall, he could have played any sport he wanted to in his high school, but he was sent to work on the docks by his drug running parents. He had rich black hair, which was tied in long dreadlocks, cascading down his back, a long black beard and eyes black as coal, that could pierce through the devil himself, if he were allowed.

He feared no one, not man nor beast. His bare-knuckled fights in Kingston, some sanctioned in seedy bars and some on the street, earned him the nick name of "Black Beard the Pirate," which was not that far off of the legendary man himself.

His real name was Lester Smith and he was called by most who knew him to his face as Captain Lester, especially by his crew. The manpower on his boat consisted of five good sailors, who were blindly loyal to him and would lay down their lives in his service, if need be.

Dressed like a pirate of yore, he wore white long pants stuffed into black leather boots, which were waterproof and had rubber soles. He had on a black cotton tank top, worn during the day in the hot sun, which showed off his large muscular frame and many tattoos. At night, when the sun began to set, he would don his red captain's jacket with fancy epaulets and brass buttons. He wore a thick black leather belt, which held his steel cutlass at his side and a second belt, with double holsters, each holding two Smith and Wesson .357 Magnum revolver pistols. They were model 686 and were made of stainless steel, better for the salty air. On his head he wore a red bandanna, tied at the back and a large black pirate's hat with three corners. He wore big hoop golden earrings and also many thick gold chains around his neck, mostly taken from his victims. He was 38 years old, the approximate age the real Blackbeard was reported to have died.

The look was not as much to be practical, as it was to inspire fear. It made him look much larger, almost seven feet in height. He smiled. He would frighten the devil out of his many victims!

He looked over at his prisoners, whom he had taken by force off their silly little American yacht. There were four of them. Two white men in their twenties and two Hispanic women, about the same age. They were sitting on the deck, shackled with their hands behind their backs. The men wore long black bathing shorts, more like surfer's trunks, and the girls wore white bikinis, which contrasted with their dark skin.

Captain Lester looked down and shook his head. He had overtaken their yacht, which should never have been in these waters. He and his crew forced themselves onto their deck, military style, and took them prisoners. His crew could have just shot them, but he had no reason to do that since they had dropped to their knees and put their hands on their heads in complete surrender. But now what was he supposed to do with them?

He wasn't into torture, killing or rape, only *money*. He would find out if they had financial resources, and if so, find a way to steal their money and get rid of them.

The fact that they could identify him made him laugh. Everyone could identify him! But try to catch him, or stop him? That was another matter completely.

He walked down the ladder off the bridge to the deck. The men and the girls had dozed off, likely due to the vast amount of alcohol they had consumed before he had commandeered their vessel and also likely from fear. He nudged the closest man with his foot on his leg. The man continued to sleep. He nudged harder and this time kept the pressure on his leg. Suddenly, the man woke up.

"What, what?" he stammered, looking up at the big man with the scary beard.

In a Jamaican accent, Captain Lester asked, "What is your name boy?"

"Archibald. Archibald!" He smiled up at the mean looking pirate. "But my friends call me Archie!"

Captain Lester stared down at him, which caused Archie to flinch and turn his head away.

"I am not your friend, *mon!*" I don't know you. I don't like you, nor your bitches either!

He reached down with great force and yanked him to his feet. At only 5'6", chubby and slow, Archibald was no match for the scary pirate.

"Do you have money, *mon?* Do you and your friends want to live?"

Archie shook his head. The others because of the commotion had been roused out of their slumber. They sat looking up at the big man who held their friend. They did not dare move, lest they suffered the same fate.

"So, you have no money, *mon?* Lester released him with a slight shove and he fell back to the deck, landing on his head and back. He saw stars and didn't move.

"How about you, *mon?*" as he looked over at the other American. "What is your name, boy?"

"Turnbull, but I go by Turner, and yes, I have money. It might be tough to retrieve it…" he started when Lester yanked him to his feet.

"Hey, hey, what are you doing?" he stammered.

Captain Lester was getting bored of this. He let him go and

he fell back onto the deck.

He looked over at two of his crewmen, who knew what his next move would be.

"Strip them."

They smiled and walked over to the four scared tourists.

The girls started screaming as their bathing suits were ripped off and the men tried to fight back as their bathing suits were pulled down past their ankles. As they lay naked in the hot Caribbean sun, Lester pulled out a long knife from the sheaf on his hip. He held it under the chin of Turner.

"We will have sex with your women while you watch, then cut off your testicles and throw you to the sharks. How much money do you have?"

Turner didn't hesitate, "One hundred and twenty-five thousand in my account." My wife has an additional fifty thousand, but her dad works for the FBI. Take the one twenty-five and let us go. I can punch it up in my phone to your account and you can drop us off at the Florida Kay. I don't want trouble. I want to live and I don't want my wife to find out I was here and not at the convention in Atlanta."

Captain Lester smiled, "I like you. You are a man of honor. Ha, Ha! I too am a man of honor. Also, I am not greedy. We will transfer your money to my account. One way only. Then we will release you. My crew looks at your girlfriends with favor, ya."

Turner looked away from the pirate. "You can have them. Spare my friend and me," at which both the girls screamed and cursed at him in Spanish.

Lester smiled again. He reached down and grabbed him by his hair and pulled his head back. Savagely, he slapped him hard across his face.

"Pig! You give up your women while you sail free? This may not turn out well for you after all. Maybe I don't like you! Have you no honor, *mon*? Do you not care about protecting the women, which is a man's duty? You are a weak, puffy bitch!"

Turner paled beneath his rich man's tan. As he lay on the deck, he could feel his face swelling up.

Lester looked at his crew, who were staring at the girls naked bodies. He sighed. No sex today. The girls were not at fault.

"Release the girls."

"Put your clothes back on," he told them. Their handcuffs were removed by the crewmen. The girls both scrambled to dress quickly, holding their tattered bathing suits against their bodies.

"Release the men too," he added. His crew released the men from their handcuffs. Neither one of them moved, nor did they cover up their nakedness.

He turned to Turner. "It is time for you to perform, *mon*. Transfer the money. When I have confirmation, we will release you."

Turner moved to try to get up to his elbows. He stared at the pirate.

"Aren't you afraid we will be able to identify you?"

Lester threw back his head and roared with laughter. He grabbed Turner's cell phone from his hand. He turned it to the "self" mode and took a picture of his own face. He tossed it to Turner.

"I am Blackbeard," he yelled, "Tell them all who I am and who hung you and your mates by my very rigging and then set yer yacht adrift! Or maybe I'll place you back aboard and be done with ye! In any case, I will have your money, which you will transfer now! Death or cash, what will it be?"

As if on cue, three of his crew, drew handguns and pointed them at the heads of the prisoners.

Turner looked down and suddenly, against his will, made the transfer. He and Archibald both pulled up their swim trunks.

Lester, checked his own phone. After five minutes, he looked up at them and smiled. "It is done. Do you want to go or do you want to die?"

He motioned that they could now board their vessel, which was tied up alongside the pirate boat.

With heads down, the four of them jumped over to their boat and cast off.

As they sailed away, Lester looked at them and smiled. He had never met an adversary he couldn't best without much trouble. Because of his size and intimidation, he never had to kill anyone, but he was not afraid to, if it was necessary.

Usually, it was all too easy. So sad. He sighed. He shook his head. The Lion King that had never met the other most feared animal in the jungle, who was still loose and looking for an adversary.

He had always hoped to one day meet that one motherfucker you never wanted to deal with. Live or die. A fight to the death for their eternal soul! Kill or be killed. Finally, to the very end.

Just once.

Just for the thrust of life and its own reward.

Just for pity's sake. For mankind's sake!

Just once. Just once.

The thought made him smile. He would find his adversary.

No matter what. He had to be out there. Who could he be?

CHAPTER ONE

THE BLUE HOLE OF THE CARIBBEAN

NINETY MILES AWAY, CAPTAIN BILL TREESE ONCE again looked down into the warm waters of the Caribbean, "Big Hole in the Ocean", or *Gran Agujero en el Océano*, as it was known locally. It was one year after the last go around at the Village of the Lost El Dorado.

Bill had gotten a little fatter. It was true he was getting older. Maybe he drank a little too much and maybe he ate a little too much, too. As for exercise, where was he going to go on an 80' Elco PT boat? The truth was, he had worked like hell to get his boat back into the water after it had nearly been sunk last year. His first mate, Manolo, had fixed the engines, repaired the damaged hull, and they both eventually replaced the ordinance, consisting of four Mark IV torpedoes, four depth charges, thousands of rounds for the Oerlikon 20 mm cannon and also the two twin .50 caliber machine guns.

His mind drifted back to that time for only a moment and

then suddenly he focused on his present circumstances. This hole in the water was estimated to be almost 500 feet deep. Others said it was over 800 feet to the bottom. Bill's sonar showed it to be a little over 500 feet.

Many had died seeking the gold and treasure reportedly within this hole. Most had returned, all with a different story. Some had died because they went too deep and stayed down too long. It was an often too familiar story, as beginning divers stayed underwater beyond the safe limits, tried to come up too fast since they had now run out of air, and suffered the "bends," or otherwise known as decompression sickness. This was where the dissolved gasses were coming out of solution into bubbles inside the body during decompression or during the ascent to the surface. It was not only painful; it could be fatal.

The Hole itself, was not purely vertical. There were some small bends and turns, but for the most part it was relatively straight down to the bottom. There were three or four ledges, or shelves on the sides, which jutted outward. These were supposedly formed by water receding during the Ice Age and then, as the ice melted and the water rose, the hole was formed.

Many ships lost at sea were reported to be down there. They were in an area known as the local "Devil's Triangle" because ships, planes and people disappeared forever. But the reality was, who really knew? There were so many legends about this place, that the unknown was far more prevalent than the truth, which was yet to be discovered.

So why go down there in the first place? Bill had asked himself that many times. The only answer he could come up with was the same reason they climbed Mt. Everest. Because it was there.

Bill had experience with deep water diving using special tanks and specially mixed gasses to support life during deep dives for extended periods of time. His two mates were Manolo, who was still with him and Miguel, who was here for the last dive, but not for the adventure up the Amazon to the Lost El Dorado.

Both young men were expert divers, who could free dive without supplemental air to over 100 feet down. When they had scuba tanks on, they could stay down deeper and longer than the average diver because of their youth and athleticism.

Miguel was going to stay on the boat as the lookout and sentry, while Bill and Manolo made the first dive. They were not going to go all out on this dive, as they had planned last year, with deep dives and decompression stops along the way, which were necessary to keep the nitrogen out of their blood and to avoid the bends. Bill had several tanks with different mixtures of gasses, which would allow them to stay down longer and dive deeper, but this was just a preliminary, surveillance dive.

Now they were going to go down to only 80 to 100 feet to look around and assess the situation. This initial dive should be an easy one for recon and surveillance. No drama. No danger. *For once*, he thought.

****

United States Navy Captain Bryce Jackson Wong, (call sign "Eagle" because of his over-the-top eyesight), a jet pilot, was about to take off from his aircraft carrier, the U.S.S. Carl Vinson. He was the CAG, or the Commander of the Air Group and was the carrier's chief pilot. He had received clearance and was going through preflight inspections in his F-35C Lightning II from Lockheed Martin, a U.S. carrier-based, singleseat, single-engine stealth combat aircraft. It was called Double Nuts, meaning it was numbered 00. He was hooked onto the catapult, which would propel him forward with high pressure steam. The flight crew raised the jet blast deflector behind his aircraft.

He received the command to take off and saluted his catapult officer, (who was nicknamed "Tommy the Shooter" because of his precise assessment of knowing how much steam pressure to apply), as he was about to be catapulted off the carrier runway. Captain Wong began to blast his plane's engine, while still being held in place, as his engine generated huge amounts of thrust. Suddenly, Tommy released the pistons and there was an explosion of steam, as the pressure slammed the plane forward. It reached the end of the deck and, as with many take offs, the plane dropped a few feet toward the ocean, until his thrusters propelled him up out of ground effect.

As he shot up, he did the peacetime maneuver of rolling his wings in a 360-degree barrel roll once as he began to reach altitude.

His mission was to recon over a Columbian base, which had apparently been sending communications to the Middle East, strictly against international protocol. He was only supposed to be in the air for 75 minutes. His wingman should have taken off a few seconds behind him, but he could hear them complaining that their catapult had broken and it was going to take a few minutes to fix it. Captain Wong was unconcerned and knew they could fix it. He continued toward his target, knowing his wingman would catch up to him.

At the 14-minute mark was when all hell broke loose.

First there was a fire warning on his engine, which he was able to mitigate by reducing power to 50 percent. Then, because of the loss of power, speed and altitude, the stall horn began chirping, meaning he had to pick up speed somehow, or he might go into a spin. These aircraft were not like the old planes, which could glide for miles. Without power, without trust, it would crash and burn almost immediately.

Captain Wong, an experienced pilot, did the next best thing he could do. In order to pick up speed and recover from the stall, he shoved the yoke forward and began to dive toward the ocean. His speed indicator showed that he was almost going fast enough to recover, but his altitude monitor showed that he was getting dangerously close to the sea and that was not good.

Suddenly his engine went dead and, looking out to the sides, he could see black smoke coming up from under his fuselage. He pulled back on the yoke to pick up any vertical altitude he could muster, using his momentum to send him upward for a few seconds.

"Mayday, Mayday," he shouted over the radio, "Fire onboard! Abandoning ship! I'm punching out!"

He pulled on the lever next to his seat and the explosion shot him clear of the aircraft, which suddenly dove down and hit the surface of the water three seconds later.

His seat arched upwards and then, began to drop to the earth. At that moment, his chute should have deployed, but it didn't.

"No Chute! No Chute!" he screamed into the transmitter

on his vest, "I'm going down! Last coordinates! Plane gone! I may be done! This is a real Charlie Foxtrot!"

At the very last second, before he hit the water, his chute deployed, cutting his speed of descent in half, but still not enough to keep most people alive.

He hit the water with a splash and went underwater. In spite of the cold and the wet, he lost consciousness. His life vest inflated and he floated to the surface, still unconscious, with his face sideways in the water, meaning he was taking in water, but also some air, which was keeping him alive.

Bill Treese was looking over the rail at the Blue Hole, when he saw the F-35C shoot over his head doing over 600 miles per hour. "Low," he thought, until it suddenly shot upward and then turned over and descended rapidly towards the water. He saw the pilot eject, seconds before the plane crashed into the ocean.

He lit up the PT boat, shouting to his crew, "We gotta' go! Right now! Right now!"

Manolo and Miguel rushed up onto the deck. They had been below making preparations for the dive.

"What is it, *Capitain?*" asked Monolo.

"It's a Navy jet that just crashed! The pilot bailed out but there was no chute until the last second. He may be dead, but we have to get there! Let's go, damnit!"

By his estimation, it was less than a mile to get to the spot of impact.

Bill shoved the throttle all the way forward. All three engines of the PT boat came to life and they shot forward, with Miguel and Manolo falling back against the day cabin, due to the force of the thrust forward. They covered the distance in less than a minute.

The crash of the pilot produced a green dye in the water, highlighting his position.

The PT boat screamed forward until they were almost on top of the pilot, who was floating, face still sideways in the water. Manolo, who had worked with Bill for years, grabbed the wheel and shouted to Bill, "*Capitain*, I've got this!"

Bill ran to the side of the PT boat. He grabbed a life lanyard attached to the boat and fastened the other end to his belt. He grabbed a life jacket and put it on.

Manolo, suddenly chopped the power to the boat, to stop the propellers from continuing to rotate, which would be dangerous to the men in the water. As they approached the pilot, Bill jumped into the water, landing just in front of the him. The wake of the PT boat slowed down and literally washed the pilot right into Bill's arms. Bill grabbed him and rolled him over onto his back. He made sure he was breathing. As the boat shot past, Manolo started the engines up and then turned the boat around, moving closer. He cut the power again, allowing it to drift. Manolo hoped he timed it right. Bill swam toward the boat, towing the pilot forward with his hand under the airman's chin. Fighting the boat's wake and the current of the ocean, Bill made it back to the PT boat in a few seconds.

Both Manolo and Miguel reached over and helped pull the pilot onto the deck of the boat and checked his breathing.

Bill climbed up onto the deck. He checked the pilot's pulse. He was breathing hard, shallow and fast.

Bill rolled him over onto his side and pushed on his chest.

Several ounces of water gushed out of his lungs and landed on the deck. The pilot began to cough furiously over and over. Manolo pounded on his back to help him expel more water.

After he stopped coughing, they rolled him over onto his back. His eyes opened and he looked around. "Where, where…?" he stammered.

Bill reached over and grasped his hand. He recognized the captain's bars on his collar.

"Captain, your plane crashed and we rescued you. We are Americans."

"Are you a U.S. flagship?" Captain Wong asked weakly.

Bill looked up at his crew, blinking a few times. He looked down at the pilot, "Uh, not exactly. Maybe seventy years ago."

"What? What? Can I please sit up?"

Bill looked at his crew and nodded. "Ok, Captain. Let's go slow, please. You hit the water pretty hard, OK?"

They sat him up and he looked around. Sitting on the deck, he could only see part of the day cabin and one of the twin .50 MM machine guns. He shook his head. "Can I please stand up?"

Bill nodded. "Ok. Let's do it slowly."

They helped Captain Wong to his feet. Blinking, he looked around. After a minute, his head began to clear. His sharp eyes didn't miss a thing.

"Ok," he said, blinking rapidly.

He saw the two twin .50 caliber Browning machine guns. He looked back at the stern, Oerlikon cannon 20 mm. He looked at the sides and back again. Four torpedo tubes, four depth charges and a smoke screen generator aft for escape from attacking WWII enemy destroyers.

He paused, "Ok, what the fuck century did I land in? I'm on a fucking PT boat! Have we already taken the Philippines, or has General MacArthur not returned yet?"

He sat back down on the deck, shaking his head back and forth, "Was I drinking before I flew last night because I never did that before?"

Bill smiled and knelt down in front of him on one knee. "Captain, let me please introduce ourselves. This is the PT 109, but only a symbolic number and homage to my hero, John Fitzgerald Kennedy. We are in the Caribbean on a treasure hunt. We are out of Columbia, but I am a veteran of the Navy, U.S.N. Captain Bill Treese, retired." He snapped off a smart salute, which Captain Wong returned with much effort. He started to say something, but Bill cut him off.

"Your jet crashed and you ejected, but the parachute did not deploy until the last second, so you hit the water pretty hard. I have contacted the Navy and they are on their way here. Until then, we are at your service. Please let me know what we can do for you until your mates arrive."

The Captain looked up at him. He closed his eyes, "Just some water please."

Bill handed him a canteen. "Don't drink a lot. Just a little."

Captain Wong drank some water. "How long?"

"They will be here in about half an hour or less. They were going to send an Angel (rescue helicopter) but decided it would be easier to get you onto a launch, since we hauled you out of the water and told them you were mostly OK. They were worried and were grateful we called them. They had tracked you and were sending out a team, but they didn't know your status."

"Ok. Thanks. I owe you my life."

"No. No, you don't. Just helping out a fellow serviceman. We don't leave anyone behind."

"Hey Bill. What was your war?"

"Vietnam."

"Ok. That's too bad. Sorry I asked."

"No. It's Ok. I've come to terms with it."

"You know, some of us in the service now...., we believe the Vietnam vets did more for the service than any other group in history."

Bill smiled, "Thanks for that. But I think the WWII guys, the WWI guys, the Korean soldiers, the Gulf guys, all might have something to say about that. But thanks. It means a lot."

Captain Wong, blinking and looking around, still in disbelief, said, "You know, I run the Navy Museum back at Pearl. Any chance of you making an appearance there for a week? We might even be able to commission the boat as an honorary Navy Vessel, full honors, of course."

Bill smiled, "Thanks. I would love to visit if we are ever in the Pacific, but the commission is not necessary. We're a bunch of civilian pirates out here," he hesitated, lest the Captain get the wrong idea, "but honest ones, of course. We help those in need, but are always on the lookout for buried treasure and new adventures. Right boys?" His crew all nodded and laughed together.

"But, having said that, it would be an honor to visit Pearl. I haven't been there in more years than I care to remember. And I would love for people to see my boat. There are only about three or four of these left in the world, and they played a huge role in

World War II. So thank you for that, also."

Captain Wong smiled and nodded, "As you wish, Captain."

Suddenly a roar in the distance caught their attention. They looked up to see a Navy transport boat flying across the water heading toward them.

"Your valet, Captain," said Bill.

The boat moved toward them and pulled up a few feet from the PT boat. Manolo caught the line tossed over to him by a navy crewman to secure the boat.

Two navy corpsmen sprang on board the PT boat and ran to the side of Captain Wong. They didn't say anything to Bill or his crew. They were 100 percent focused on their captain. They weren't rude, but were just tending to business. Carefully, they helped him to his feet. They brought him to the side and helped him into the Navy vessel.

Captain Wong looked back at Bill. "Thank you, Captain Treese, for saving my life. I owe you."

Bill smiled at him. "No, you don't. We are even."

Captain Wong looked back at him. He looked into Bill's eyes. "I owe you!" And with that, the boat cast off, picking up speed as they headed back to the aircraft carrier.

****

Bill and Manolo were preparing for their dive into the Hole. They had on their regular tanks, regulators and face masks. This dive was for exploration only, not scheduled to go below 100 feet. Miguel at the helm of the PT boat expertly maneuvered it to just the inner lip of the Hole, which was over 1,000 feet across and over 500 feet deep.

Miguel had been briefed on the dive and was holding the PT 109 in place using both the side thrusters and the aft engines. The original PT 109, skippered by John F. Kennedy, the future President of the United States, was sunk in the South Pacific during World War II. But Bill Treese, who rescued this boat off the scrap heap many years ago, renamed it after his hero's boat.

Bill and Manolo, standing in the stern of the boat, made their final arrangements. They both had white drawing slates on their wrists, with waterproof pens so that they could communicate. They had planned to use more sophisticated communication gear on deeper, more complicated dives. For now, they just wanted to see what was below. The boat was over the rim of the Hole, so they could use the sides as a reference after they dove in.

They didn't expect to see much.

At the 12:00 noon mark, as planned, they both leaped into the ocean, while holding their masks and regulators to their face, so they would not be ripped off from the impact of the water.

When they hit the water, they floated for a minute, as they had inflated their buoyancy control vests. They both made the OK sign and, holding the exhale tube of their buoyancy control devices over their heads, pressed the plunger to purge the air. Slowly, they descended into the gigantic hole in the middle of the ocean.

The water was slightly cold, but they knew their bodies would acclimate in a few minutes. Holding their noses to regulate the air pressure to their ears then slowly turned vertical and began to kick downward.

They descended down the side of the wall which was rough

and likely the remanent of a lava tube from an extinct volcano, or possibly a giant sink hole. At every 20 feet, they stopped, turned 360 degrees and looked around. They had twin powerful dive lights strapped to both side of their heads, each shined up to 20,000 lumens underwater, which they could dim at will, allowing the best possible penetration. They were maintaining their positions, as well as looking for predators, such as sharks, moray eels, or even jelly fish, which could be lethal depending on the type and the amount present.

They were both surprised at the visibility, over 100 feet. The water was clear and there were many species of fish swimming around. Light from above still penetrated the depths. Sunfish, bluegills, nurse sharks, tiger sharks and white tip reef sharks circled around. They were near but showed no aggressiveness. Bill was in the lead and Manolo behind and slightly to his left. They continued their descent.

Manolo, seeing an opening just below them, which looked to be about three feet high and four feet across, swam up next to Bill and touched his arm. Bill looked back and Manolo pointed to the opening. He swam up next to it, but Bill, the more experienced diver, reached out and grabbed Manolo's arm as he was about to touch the top of the opening. Manolo looked at him and Bill shook his head. "Nooo!" he said around his regulator. He paused and pulled Manolo away from the opening. Bill shown his dive light inside. His light reflected off the grinning teeth of a moray eel, its head the size of a softball! It seemed very happy to see them, but Mondo suddenly grew cold, realizing it could have bitten off his hand, had Bill not stopped him from reaching onto the ledge. He shivered and looked at Bill. His eyes said, "Thank you!" Bill winked at him through his mask and they continued their descent, until they reached the 65-foot mark. That's when they saw it.

The visibility was less but still over 70 feet, and sunlight penetrated this deep in the Hole. Lying on a ledge, jutting out into the canyon, was the unmistakable bow spar of a sailing vessel. It only came out about one foot and would have been easily overlooked, had not the deep silt, which covered the rest of the vessel, not been swept away by the current. They both increased the penetration of their dive lights.

It was covered in barnacles and other marine life, but was obviously man-made.

Bill and Manolo felt the intense thrill of discovery. Inwardly, they both also knew this vessel should have been discovered many years ago, as thousands of divers had been down here before them. But, as they also knew, the water can play tricks on your vision and, had the sunlight not been shining directly on the reflective marine life, they could have easily overlooked it.

Bill wrote on his slate, "Keep close. We have plenty of time and air. Don't rush!"

Manolo, gave him the OK sign.

They moved closer. Bill ascertained the vessel was over 100 feet long, maybe more. It was resting on its side. They swam below the spar to the bow. Bill used his hand to brush the silt aside. There was only rough, hewn wood. He could not find the name of the vessel, even though he moved a lot of silt off the sides. Whatever was there to identify the ship, was lost to the ravages of time.

He motioned forward and they both swam slowly to the center of the foredeck. The boat was on its side, with the port side facing up. It was obviously a sailing vessel, probably from the 19th century, but there were no masts. As they moved over the foredeck, Bill felt across with his hands. Manolo did the same, until he felt the rough edges of what was probably the anchor of the mast of the foredeck.

Because there was no mast, but there was a hole where it had been, it was likely the boat lost the mast when it sank or maybe that is what was part of the reason it did sink in the first place. They were in the local area of this part of the world's "Devil's Triangle." Not the more famous cousin which was near Bermuda, but dangerous and notorious, none the less.

They proceeded towards the midship. Bill was searching for a hatch to one of the holds. The ship was remarkably intact, considering it was probably well over 100 years old, but they could not see the bottom half of the ship, which could be missing.

Suddenly, Bill spotted a large ball resting on the opposite, or the starboard side of the vessel, laying in the sand. They both swam down to discover, what looked like the ship's bell! It was half buried in the sand which covered the bottom rail of the ship, as though it had been violently detached during a storm or a fight. Bill tried to brush the sand away, but it was stuck in the seafloor. It was at least two feet across and over two feet high. They both brushed the sand and silt off the base. As they continued to work, they discovered it was indeed the ship's bell. They could see it was a heavy bronze bell that had turned a green patina color.

They could just make out the name, which was also partially buried, *JAMAICAS REVENGE.* They both looked at each other. It probably weighed over two hundred pounds and they would need to come back for it later.

As they probed along the deck, Bill's dead reconning skills came into play, as he found the open hatch amidship. He shined his powerful searchlight into the hold of the vessel. The water was murky. He looked at Manolo and signaled to him to bring up the line he was carrying in his buoyancy control vest pocket. He lashed the 100-foot rope to a metal deck cleat, which easily could have pulled loose because of the age of the vessel. Unfortunately, it was the best they had.

Bill erased his easel. He wrote, "Watch out below for things that might eat you!"

Manolo nodded and gave the OK sign.

Slowly, they both descended head first into the open hold. There was no hatch, having long been lost to the ravages of the sea.

As they descended into the hold, they shone their lights around in all directions, as their lights on their heads shone straight ahead and helped to light up the hold.

They swam around moving vertically and moved back to back in 360-degree circles.

They moved forward and down into the next hold, one deck below. Bill gently tugged onto the line, which was still holding tight. The worst thing for a diver was to become disorientated in a cave or a wreck and lose his or her bearings. Without a guide to get out, they could become lost until their air was exhausted and they died.

Again, they saw nothing. They swam aft, or backward to where they thought the captain's quarters might be. Traditionally, it was in the stern of the vessel, with the officers and the medical doctor on either side. This was because it was the most stable part of the ship. The petty officers were at midship and the crew slept in bunks on the forecastle in the bow of the ship.

Here, the passage was narrow and they had to move forward in a single file. Since the ship was laying on its side, any officer's quarters they found would either be below them or above their heads. Some of the passageway, had been either demolished or disintegrated by seaworms. They were just about at the end of the passageway, which widened to the sides of the vessel, without separating walls. This was obviously the captain's quarters, but was now open to the rest of the vessel. The outer walls had begun to disintegrate.

Bill looked at his air level, which was down to 920 pounds. He held his instrument up to Manolo and tapped it. Manolo moved forward and showed he still had over 1400 pounds of air left. Bill shook his head. *Damn kids and their damn lungs,* he thought. *The boy could stay down here another two days! Jeeze!*

He moved around, feeling along the floor and then towards the back stern, looking for any signs of treasure or anything else of value.

Suddenly, he saw it under a bunch of debris, which had fallen from the deck above. A small black box, either steel or iron, reinforced with copper bands and a lock on the cover.

Reaching under the pile of wood, he suddenly pulled his hand back. He had almost placed his outreached fingers into the jaws of a moray eel! Its head was the size of a small dog and it showed very large teeth. He had no idea how long it was, but it didn't matter.

He pulled back and motioned for Manolo, who swam up. His eyes got big. Bill motioned for him to bring up the shark stick, which would detonate a 12-gauge shotgun shell on contact. But in the small space they were in, the shotgun blast could be dangerous for them and could damage what was left of the rear of the ship. So, Bill actually turned it around and gently probed the eel with the handle, until it moved back into its hole, deeper into the debris. Bill then quickly reached in and grabbed the box, which was about three feet long by two feet deep and two feet high. The lid was rounded, like a treasure chest.

It was heavy, which was a good sign. Tucking it under his left arm, he used his right hand to move along the rope line back to the surface of the ship. They both had their dive lights on very bright settings, but only enough to penetrate the dark hold of the ship. Once they were out of the vessel and back on deck, Manolo detached the cable from the metal deck cleat, and they started their slow ascent to the surface, both anxious to see what was in the box.

CHAPTER TWO

A PIRATE'S TALE AND THE CURSE

CAPTAIN LESTER, KNOWN TO MANY IN THESE waters as Blackbeard the Pirate, leaned against the side of the bridge bulkhead. His first mate Trinidad steered the boat across the gentle waters of the Southern Caribbean. Although, technically, they were nearer the north coast of Brazil, they were still in Caribbean waters, as they saw it.

It was nearing midnight and the air sea rescue boat plowed through the waters, heading for their home base of Trinity Island.

He thought about the two young couples he had robbed earlier that day. *What pansies, he thought. Willing to give up their women? Money yes. Easy come, easy go. Who cares? A fat popinjay like that could make the money back in a week. But to let two pretty young girls come to harm, because he was no man, was inexcusable. And to make it worse, he said, 'please don't let my wife know. Her dad is an FBI agent.'*

He shook his head and laughed to himself. *His father-in-law might know more than he thinks! If he's screwing around on his baby, he may find out that hanging from Blackbeard's yardarms would be a better fate for him! Ho, Ho!*

He looked up at the evening sky and the million plus stars of the Southern Cross. The boat plowed forward, sending occasional sprays of salty water into his face.

He looked over at his first mate Trinidad, who had been with him since they were young men back in Jamaica.

"Trinidad! What you think about them pansies, *mon?*"

Trinidad looked at his friend and captain, "Typical fluffy white boys captain! They fat, ya! Give away their money and their women to protect their fluffy baby asses!"

They both laughed.

"A mi fi tell yu! Ya, *mon,*" started Captain Lester, "you right, but you liked those girls. I could see it in your eyes!"

"I know. Forgive me. I, like you, am not into the abuse of women or children." His voice drifted off. "It's just been a long while since I lost my Mary…". He looked down, "You know Lester," he said dropping the formally of Captain.

"Yes, my friend. It was the sickness that took her suddenly and that of your baby inside her."

Trinidad took a long breath. Like Captain Lester, he was a big man, over 6'2" and weighed 250 lbs. He played rugby back in Jamaica, and he and Lester were fast friends. They liked being pirates for the money and the adventure, but sometimes they both wish they had chosen a different path.

"I am still a man after all and you know, the sight of pretty young girls, they girls were *goodaz,* ya, still arouses me, but," he added, "not in that way. Let the beasts of the world rape and burn and then they, themselves, can burn in hell for their very deeds!"

Lester nodded. "Breathe easy, *mon.*" He looked up at the

stars. They would be at their island in less than two hours.

"So, Captain, you have spoken many times about the treasure your great grandpa liberated and then hid somewhere in these islands. He did big *tings,* ya? Tell me again, what do you know?"

Captain Lester took a long breath. When he related a long story, he would drop his Jamaican slang and could speak in almost perfect English.

"It was in the middle of the Civil War in the U.S. The Confederates were putting up a huge resistance in the Charleston Harbor and the Union offered them money to buy the services of the mercenaries from Jamaica, they were going to hire to break the blockade.

"Mi great grandpa, from Jamaica, promised them that the men they hired would be in place, but then he had heard from his spies that the Union generals were not going to pay them at all. Once the small advance money changed hands, the Union soldiers were to place mi great grandpa under arrest for treason, but not tell the Jamaican soldiers who were fighting for what they thought was Union money. The end result would be, the Union got the Jamaican mercenaries to attack the blockade, the Union kept the money and the Union hung mi great grandpa and his people for treason so they would never talk."

"So, what happened?"

"Mi great grandpa got paid the gold he was promised, ya. When they came to capture him and throw him in jail, he killed them bastards and pulled back his people, so there was never an attack on the Confederates."

"*Dat shot, mon,*" said Trinidad, "Good for him, ya!"

"It took a lot of gumption on mi great grandpa's part because, like us, he was black and did not believe in the slavery. So, he wanted to support the Union. But they were deceitful and they too, hated blacks, but they didn't say it. Everyone hated us back then. The North had their own reasons for abolishing slavery and it wasn't because they thought it was a bad thing!"

They were both silent. Finally, Trinidad said, "And what of the treasure?"

Captain Lester looked at the approaching clouds, knowing it was going to be a storm at some point. He looked at Trinidad. "According to mi family, it is located on the island we are living on. While we have not really searched for it lately, I feel it is now time for us to do some exploring in and around the steep mountains and cliffs we are camped near.

"Since it is not a big island, we should be able to cover it in a few days. But it is possible it might be on another island around here, which can be a problem, ya."

"Weh yuh ah seh Captain?" (What are you saying?)

Captain Lester smiled. "When we get back, *memba mi tell yu,* mi great grandpa's diary and a map he drew up. It is old and broken, but it was given to me by mi grandpa, his son. Since *mi* mum and pops were not the best of people, *mi* grandpa only trusted it to me before he passed. He said to look at this island, but then go below it, under it and between it, whatever that should mean, *mon.*" He shrugged, "The blind whispering of an old man on his death bed."

Trinidad nodded.

"That's what we seek, *mon,*" said Blackbeard.

****

Once Bill and Manolo reached the PT boat, it was getting to be late afternoon. The sun was still hot, but the seas were picking up and they knew they had to get back to shore. The weather was turning bad and there was a storm brewing. Plus, they were beginning to run low on food and fuel, the two things they could not be without.

Miguel helped them aboard. They took off their scuba gear and dropped it on the deck. After he pulled off his fins, Bill grabbed his tank and Manolo's tank and placed them in the rack on the side of the stern deck. They needed to be refilled, but not now. He had set down the box on the deck, which Miguel saw immediately. He smiled.

"So *Capitain*, how was your first dive?" He smiled again.

"Productive, Miguel, productive. But we will see if it is full of sea water or a million dollars in gold doubloons!"

Manolo smiled, but then looked concerned. "*Capitain* Bill. We should take it below deck to your quarters or the galley. Too many eyes may be looking here, *comprende*?"

Bill nodded. "Good point boys." With that he kicked off the rest of his gear and, bending low, he picked up the chest, which was actually fairly heavy, and made his way down the ladder to the galley. Once there, he placed the chest on the sea dining table, where there was more room than in his small cabin.

Manolo, having shed his diving gear, also joined him.

"Miguel is driving the boat. He says we will make shore in about four to five hours. There is a storm which will hit about midnight and we need to be tied to a dock in a sheltered harbor to ride it out. It is too dangerous out here, *Capitain* Bill."

Bill was nodding, but not really hearing him. He was focusing on the box in front of him. He did not expect a booby trap, which would blow up, because they found it in what was presumably the captain's quarters and likely his own strong box. It could contain the crew's payroll, or possibly weapons or even valuable trinkets of gold and silver. The ships were also carrying gold bars, but those would be heavier, he thought, than the box he lifted out of the ship. But you never really knew until you opened it up.

Bill was studying the lock, which seemed complex, but maybe not impossible.

Manolo looked on in silence. He had seen his friend working before when he was trying to solve a riddle, or, as in this case, untie a knot.

Bill, seated at the table, turned the box on its back, looking straight down on the lock. It looked like it could be opened with a simple skeleton key, but he knew that was too simple. He looked all around it, as if there might be another way in.

He shook the box gently, to see if there was something inside that might be sliding around, but there was nothing. Frowning, he went to the lock and tried to open it using his fingers, but it would not budge.

He went to his cabin and returned with a skeleton key he had in his sea desk. Trying to insert it, it only went a quarter of the way into the lock then it stopped.

Bill pulled out his Swiss Army knife and tried various tools with no success.

Because of the heat below deck, he had broken out in a

sweat; the salty rivulets pouring off his face and dropping onto his shirt and pants.

Finally, he gave up. Leaning back in his chair, he said to Manolo, "Do we still have some hand grenades? Getting tired of this."

"No *Capitian*. Do you want me to try?"

Bill smiled, "Sure Manolo," appeasing his young mate, "but remember this is a very complicated lock."

Manolo pulled a bobby pin from his long hair, a simple pocket knife with a single thin blade from his pocket and began to use them on the lock.

Bill continued, "It is also very old and rusty and probably needs to be…" was all he could say, as the lid of the box popped open when Manolo twisted his blade inside the lock.

Bill's eyes went wide as he said, "Wait, how did you..?"

"It's OK, *Capitain*. It's not the first time I had to break into a lock." He smiled.

Bill shook his head in disbelief. "Unbelievable," he said to no one in particular.

"Ok, let's see what is in this thing."

The first thing they noticed was the contents were dry. No water had seeped inside. There was a brown cloth covering the contents, which Bill pulled off. It was heavy and some kind of oilskin. Underneath was an equally heavy red cloth, which he also removed. Eagerly they looked inside.

Bill caught his breath as Manolo gasped in surprise. Lying in the middle was a large, ornate gold cross, embedded with blue and green jewels, probably sapphires and jade. It was over a foot long. There was a heavy gold chain attached to it. Bill lifted it out. The cross was thick and the chain was about 20 inches in length. There were four solid gold bars lying next to the cross. Bill pulled them out. They probably weighed around two pounds each and had smooth, rounded edges. There were several gold doubloons, maybe 20 scattered around with crosses on the front and several letters and lines on the back. There were also seven gold medallions, with figures of a woman on the front and, again letters and symbols on the back. It didn't appear there were dates on them, so other than the pure weight and value of the metal, there was no way to put a numismatic value on them.

As Bill removed the pieces one by one, he discovered a second oil cloth covering up another layer below. He lifted up the cloth and, again, caught his breath. There were three heavy hand daggers, each almost two feet long, with gold handles, richly adorned with jewels, pearls and what appeared to be abalone shell. The sheaths covering the blades, were also made of thick gold and richly adorned. As Bill drew out the swords, one by one, it appeared the blades were stainless steel, still shiny yet and covered with etchings of words, some in Spanish, some in an unknown language and symbols of animals and unholy beasts.

Bill went back to his cabin and brought out a large magnifying glass, which had a light attached to it. Looking closely at one of the daggers, he began reading the inscription on the blade, which were in Spanish. Suddenly, Bill drew his breath in sharply. The hairs on the back of his neck stood up on their own. He unwittingly dropped all three of the daggers back into the box and crossed himself several times. He stood up and pushed himself away from the table. He began to breath heavily, almost wheezing as though he was suffering from an asthma attack.

Manolo, never seeing his skipper in this state of mind, also took a step back.

"*Capitain*, what is it? What did we find?"

"The Devil, Manolo. Somehow, the Devil has found us once again."

****

The PT boat had been running for over two hours. Because of the heavy current, it was going to take them almost five hours to make it to land and their safe harbor.

Bill was at the helm. He had recovered from his shock at the artifacts they had found and his rational mind had taken over.

Bill had told Manolo to contact Bill's friend, Dr. John Waales, a professor of archelogy at U.C. Berkeley, and tell him what they had found. Manolo had sent a couple of photos to him via text, but not many because of the sensitive nature of what they were doing. It had taken awhile for the satellite links to reach John Waales and then more time for him to get back to them.

John had recommended a secure link up through his own communication system, which he used with other professors and other universities, so that their data could not be hacked. With Bill's permission, Manolo sent all of the pictures he had taken of the artifacts and from many different angles. He told the Professor that they were making for land due to the nature of the storm. John had said to give him 12 hours and contact him in the morning if they could, depending on the atmospherics of the storm.

Manolo relayed this to Bill, who nodded in affirmation and told him to let John know they would do as he asked. By the time they reached the port, it was full dark and they were all starving. They pulled up to the dock and tied the boat down fore and aft. Because of the storm, they put out several rubber bumpers between the boat and the dock, to protect the sides of the boat against a heavy current. The port was familiar to them and they knew they were not in any danger. They also knew that everything, including the food service would be closed up, due to the storm, so Manolo had made beans, rice and poached fish in mango sauce, which they all gobbled up like starving men.

Bill pulled out some Havana Club Rum and shared it with his crew. The liquor went down well. It was fiery, but very smooth, almost like a rich brandy. After a couple of drinks, they all went on deck, secured the weapons and locked away the ordinance. It was starting to rain and they knew they were in for a long night. Finally, after a long and successful day, they all went to sleep, happily without a sentry for a change, while the rain and the winds increased to almost gale force strength.

The morning brought a monsoon-like rain. The winds whipped over the island, causing morning to appear like night due to the nature of the cloud cover.

Bill, Manolo and Miguel, feeling like fat tourists, all slept in, knowing they were safe in this harbor. Finally, Manolo, with a pinch of guilt, got up at 0800 and headed for the galley. Pulling out eggs, bacon, biscuits and pancake mix, he began to whip up a large breakfast for everyone.

Bill and Miguel continued to sleep, until the unmistakable smell of sizzling bacon and coffee began to force its way through the holds of the boat.

Manolo was cooking until he heard the sound of Bill's hatch opening up with a hard scrape against the deck. Manolo smiled and immediately poured Bill a large cup of hot, black coffee and set it on the galley table.

Bill, wandering towards the table, sniffed loudly, looking at the table. He blinked twice.

"Manolo?"

"Good morning *Capitain*. Time for a good breakfast!"

"No chilies today," Manolo added, "just your American boring stuff!" He smiled.

Bill let himself down into the chair at the table in front of the coffee. He drank almost the entire cup in one gulp.

"Ah, that's good! Can I have a little more, please?"

Manolo knew his captain well. He immediately brought over the almost full pot of coffee and poured it to the brim.

Setting down the pot, he shoved a full plate of food in front of his captain. Bill smiled, "Biscuits and gravy, bacon, eggs over-easy, pancakes and coffee. Does it get any better than this? Thanks Manolo! Nobody can outdo you in the galley, son!"

Manolo smiled. Next came Miguel, wiping his eyes and yawning loudly, and Manolo repeated the same scenario for him as well.

They all sat around the table, lingering over coffee and scraps of food, because, quite frankly, there was nothing else to do while the storm raged overhead.

Bill stood up and drained his third cup of Manolo's black, rich Columbian coffee. He set the cup down on the table. "Ok. Time to call John and invite him out for the party!"

Manolo looked up. "*Capitain*, is Kimmi done with her

studies?" he asked earnestly, while Miguel laughed into his own coffee cup.

Manolo shot him a quick look with a frown.

Bill smiled. "Yes Manolo. She graduated with honors from U.C. Berkeley. Archaeology, just like her pops. I have no doubt, she is dying to return to the luxuries of a greasy PT boat and its greasy captain and crew! To do research, of course!" he added hastily.

"No *Capitain!* I bathe daily!" He looked over at Miguel, who was chortling at his friend's obvious love for this American girl, "Unlike some stinky crewmen who don't shower..., ever!" Manolo added.

This sent them all into peals of laughter, as Manolo's true feelings for Professor John Waales' daughter was revealed to them.

The laughter died down and Manolo, looking off in the distance, as though looking at her, said, "It would be nice to see her again."

He smiled and looked down. "I think I love her."

Miguel smiled respectfully and said no more.

Bill said nothing, but got up and headed for the bridge to assess the weather. Inwardly, he hoped Kimmi would know that she could look for the rest of her life and not find a better man who could come close to the love Manolo would give her. He shook his head. Once love presented its face to you, you had better grab and hold on because it may never find you again. He put on his foul weather raincoat and floppy rain hat, then stepped up the ladder to the deck and into the storm.

Professor John Waales was in his office on the campus

of U.C. Berkeley when the phone rang. He was located in the Life Science Building or LSB, as it was affectionately known on campus. It was located off Sproul Plaza, which was made famous in 1964-1965 by the Free Speech Movement, a massive student protest, under the leadership of Mario Savio. This was the first major and notorious act of civil disobedience on an American college campus in the 1960s.

John turned from his computer, where he was imputing data from his last trip to the Amazon.

He picked up his cell phone and recognized the familiar number of his friend Bill Treese.

"Ahoy, Captain Bill, what are you about today?" he said in sailor speak.

"Hi, John. Are you ready to come down here? We found some goodies." his voice fell off.

"Yes, of course. I've been studying them and doing some research. I don't have a lot of answers for you yet. But I will have some data soon. What do you need me to bring?"

"I'll text you, John," was Bill's reply. "It might get a little rough. Is Jack available?" he said hopefully, meaning Dr. Jack Paris, John's chiropractor and close personal friend, who had helped them on their last two adventures up the Amazon River.

"Yes. I already spoke to him and he wants to go."

"What about your daughter Kimmi?"

"No doubt she would want to come, but against my better judgment! As always." He sighed, "She's packing her bags even as we speak."

Bill smiled, then continued, "Did you see the hieroglyphics and the ancient symbols on the blades of the daggers? I've seen them somewhere before, but I can't put my hands on it. I just remember they were not good things. Pretty sure they were about sacrifices and devil worship in pagan lands or during pagan times. Maybe medieval or possibly before the birth of Jesus."

John said, "With your permission, I would like to show them to a close colleague of mine, here at the university, who studies the world of ancient devil worship and supernatural deities. He is an excellent source and will save me three or four weeks of research. Plus, he will play it close to the vest and will not reveal who asked him to look into this."

"Yes," said Bill, "if you trust him, that is good enough for me. When will you guys be able to be here?"

"We are making preparations to fly out today, in about eight hours. The flight is to Miami, then to you on a connection. However, due to your storm, which I am sure you are enjoying at this very moment, we may have a spot of bother, getting to you," he said with a slight British accent, just to be funny.

Bill, sitting in his small cabin on the PT boat, looked up and listened to the wind howl and the heavy rain strike his deck above him. He was monitoring the weather on his CB radio weather band, but it did not show an end to the storm. Nor was his radar telling him anything, except there was a massive cloud all around them.

"Yeah, John, it could be a bit of a problem, unless it breaks. We are here for the duration, until you get here. Nowhere to go. When you get to Miami, call me and let me know what is going on with your connecting flight. We will hire a jeep to come and get you and bring you to the boat."

"Sounds like a plan. See you in a day or two!"

Bill put down his phone. He leaned back in his chair. He looked at the treasure chest, wondering if it would lead to good things or bad things. *Did I inadvertently open Pandora's Box? he thought,* with a slight amount of amusement mixed with fear.

****

Bill had to wait almost 48 hours to pick up John, Kimmi and Jack at the airport, due to the constant pounding of the storm, which finally let up enough, so that their small twin prop plane could land. They had had to stay in the Miami airport for almost 12 hours, waiting for the clearance to come, indicating it was safe to fly out.

Bill and Manolo were waiting for them in the small Quonset hut at the airfield. It was controlled airspace, meaning there was a tower where plane landings and takeoffs were being controlled, but there was no comfortable airport terminal, with a bar and restaurant.

Once the plane arrived, Bill and Manolo were allowed onto the tarmac to greet them. Hugs were given all around; Kimmi and Manolo, hugged and kissed each other.
Overcome with love and passion, they could barely contain themselves. This was not lost on the others, especially her father John, who inwardly realized he may have lost a daughter, but may have gained a fine son-in-law somewhere along the way. He sighed. It was OK.

They made it back to the boat in less than an hour, stowed their gear aboard, and set sail for the Blue Hole.

Bill took them below, with Miguel at the helm and showed

them all the treasure, he and Manolo had brought up from the wreck in the Hole.

Jack whistled in amazement. "Wow. This is amazing! Do you know the name of the ship or how long she has been down there?"

Bill nodded his head. "Yes and no. It is ***JAMAICAS REVENGE***, but no idea how long it has been down there. I was hoping you guys might help us find some answers."

John spoke up, "I have some vague theories, but they mostly lead to more questions, as they often do."

Bill looked up. "What about your colleague? Was he able to help?"

"Sort of," said John. "When I showed him the photos, he was clearly taken aback and shall I say, very disturbed. He said they were ancient and evil. He couldn't elaborate, but would do some research and get back to me.

"Scary. I never saw him act that way before. It was almost as though I had brought a curse on him and now he had to figure out a way to survive. Crazy! We are men of science! Not supposed to listen to a lot of superstitious nonsense!"

Bill was thoughtful. "Yes, you are right. But we have seen things out here that we cannot explain." His voice drifted off.

For a moment, they all thought about the girl, Zenadia, who they had encountered last year. She had superhuman powers, which had affected them all.

Bill continued, "Did he give you any direction as to the origin of the symbols, or what they mean? The Spanish I understand, but what about the rest of the markings?"

"Yes." Slowly, John pulled out a folded piece of paper from

his pocket. He unfolded it and, holding it up to the light, began to read. *"These daggers represent death. Death to all the unbelievers, who do not swear loyalty to our supreme leader, Lucifer our Lord! We will not rest, we will not stop, we will not quit, until you have been found and punished. If you hold these words in your hands and you are an unbeliever, you have now been cursed for all time. There is no hope for you."*

They were all silent, especially Bill.

Kimmi, Jack, John and Manolo all looked at Bill, whose eyes were wide open. "Yikes!" he said. "That can't be good."

Jack, dropping into his best Bill Murray imitation from "Ghost Busters", suddenly said, "Woe! Woe! Bad guys are coming for me! Woe, woe! I'm not afraid! Woe, woe! Who 'ya gonna call? Devil Busters!" He paused, "Fuck 'em! He smiled. "Sorry. Can't take this shit too seriously or it will drive you crazy! And I ain't afraid of no ghosts!"

No one said anything. It was an awkward silence.

Finally, John spoke up. "We've all been through a million things worse than this so far. Yes, we can get geeked out by it, but what the hell? I've seen things down here that I could never explain in the real world we come from. So let's say there is a curse on Bill or us? Let's keep moving forward with our plan. Like you, Jack, I ain't afraid of no goats! Sorry, no ghosts, either!"

They all laughed.

Bill said, matter-of-factly, "There is a lot more to worry about out here than ancient curses on swords. I will take it seriously, in that it adds and extra layer of caution on the caution I am always showing, whenever we dive or go into situations which may be dangerous. By nature, I am not superstitious, but I do believe in God, who is great and Satan, who is bad. So I will place these swords in a place in my mind and try to control my emotions concerning them. Whoever had them before us, likely knew about what they were and where they had come from. I doubt the captain of the ***JAMAICAS REVENGE*** was afraid of them and we shouldn't be either."

Bill looked around and they were all nodding. They had picked up cooked food before they left the coastal village to eat on the way to the PT boat, and Bill could see they were all tired from their travels. He continued, "If anyone wants a snack or a drink before going to sleep, ask now. But I recommend you all get some shut-eye. It'll be dawn in a few hours and we will be near the Hole. We will dive in the afternoon, once we get there."

Kimmi spoke up, "Just some water please, Uncle Bill." The rest of them nodded and they all took their gear to their respective bunks. In less than an hour, they were all asleep. Bill and Manolo climbed the ladder to the Bridge. Bill asked Manolo and Miguel to check the engines, the hull and all of the weapons. After that, they could hit their bunks as well. He asked Miguel to relieve him at 0700 and for Manolo to start breakfast around that time.

The next morning at 0700, Miguel appeared on the deck to relieve Bill, who was pretty groggy, but needed to study the charts for a while, to measure their descent and how much air and gas they would need for their scuba tanks. Miguel had slept badly once Bill had filled him in on what was going on with the swords and the dive the next day. He never wanted to show he was afraid, but he was from the Amazon Basin, and his older relatives whispered about the evil things which lived in the jungles, where they came from. He focused on driving the boat to the Hole. That kept his mind from wandering.

They had gotten their calculations for the dive from Bill. It was going to be Jack, Bill, Manolo, Kimmi and John.

Kimmi had become an experienced diver, as had her dad, John in the past year, diving several times in Monterey Bay and Carmel, off the California coast. They had done both boat dives and also shore dives. They had ventured near the deadly canyons on the edge of the kelp beds, which plunged down over 10,000 feet and allowed cold, deep-water to rise to the surface, bringing up plankton, which was fed on by the predators of Monterey Bay. Many divers had lost their lives off Monastery Beach because of the upwelling and also the deep-water currents, which pulled inexperienced divers down several hundred feet, into the canyons. Then they suddenly realized they were almost out of air and tried to dump their weight belts and shoot to the surface where there was air. Unfortunately, they suffered the bends and would die without treatment in a hyperbaric, decompression chamber. Because the water was cold, dark and full of currents, it was not the easiest place to dive. However, the beauty and visibility of the Point Lobos State Natural Reserve was second to none. But because of the adversity and inherent danger, they had to learn their craft well, becoming experienced divers very quickly.

Miguel was going to drive the boat. He too could dive and would help out, but someone needed to stay topside. He was good at piloting the boat and would also be a formidable opponent if they were ever attacked on board the PT boat. The plan was to go in early that afternoon. It was 11:00 a.m. The seas were calm and would remain that way for the rest of the day.

****

The BWM Super Motor Yacht approached the PT boat suddenly at noon. It was a luxury yacht 100 feet long and two decks above water. It could go up to 70 miles per hour. There was reggae music blasting out of the speakers.

Bill had gone below earlier, for some much-needed shut eye, as he had been up all night driving the boat. Jack was on the port gun and John on the starboard. Miguel was fixing a small leak in the engine compartment, which was more annoying than dangerous, but was letting in some sea water, none the less. Manolo was looking through the binoculars at the surrounding sea, while Kimmiko was steering the boat. It was her first time and she was having fun.

Manolo watched the yacht approach, but did not sound out general quarters, as it appeared to be a civilian party boat.

"Who are they, Manolo?" asked Kimmiko.

"I don't know. But there are several people dancing on the top deck in bathing suits and most of the girls are topless."

The boat approached and the captain or first mate shouted out over a hand-held megaphone "Attention, PT boat, we mean no harm! Just a chance to get to know you better!"

John offered, "Better get Bill up here quickly! Get Miguel up too."

Kimmi ran below and knocked on the captain's hatch, "Captain Treese, you need to come topside." She looked back toward the engine room and called for Miguel, who scrambled up the ladder leading from the engine room to the stern deck. He stayed by the Oerlikon cannon, just in case, but ready to come forward if needed.

Kimmi ran back to the bridge.

"I have alerted the captain. I don't know what these people are doing out here and why they want to see us," she said to Manolo.

"You would if you saw them dancing on deck," he smiled, looking out at the half naked girls.

Kimmi elbowed him suddenly in the ribs. She grabbed the binoculars out of his hand. "You steer the boat and I'll do the spying!"

Manolo giggled and responded good naturedly, 'Ok Kimmi!" He smiled.

Bill, rubbing his eyes, came up on deck. He saw the boat approaching. He reached into the cabinet under the bridge and pulled out his megaphone. Above the sounds of the engine and the blare of reggae music, he shouted at the approaching boat, "Party Boat! Belay that! Stand your ground! Do not approach or you will be fired on!"

He turned to Jack and John. Because the PT boat was facing them directly, they both had a clear shot at the approaching boat, which had not slowed its approach, either because they hadn't heard Bill or because they had bad intentions.

Bill yelled to Jack and John, "Give 'em a warning. Fire a volley over their heads! But way over their heads. Don't hit the people!"

Both Jack and John racked their twin .50 caliber machine guns. They both let loose a volley of fire over the top of the approaching boat that could only mean one thing; the next shots would be lethal.

The approaching boat made a sudden right turn and, continuing to turn in a 360-degree circle, stopped dead in the water facing the PT boat approximately 100 yards away. Their position put them on the PT boat's port side.

Bill called out again, "State your business, but do not, I repeat, do not come any closer or you will be fired upon!"

The person who answered him was obviously the captain of the vessel. "Captain, we mean you no harm." The music had stopped and the people on board who had been dancing had suddenly gone below decks. "We wish only to meet with you and discuss a business proposition."

Bill looked over at John and then Jack. He saw Miguel in the stern by the cannon. "Miguel, get on the cannon and swing it towards their vessel but don't fire please." Miguel moved over to the Oerlikon cannon and, grabbing the handles, turned toward the yacht and leveled the weapon at it.

Bill continued, "You can send over a boat with only the captain aboard and one sentry.

"Make sure you are unarmed," he added. "You want to parley, that is fine, but on my terms."

It took about 15 minutes, but then they saw a hard shelled, 12-foot Zodiac, with a 75 HP Mercury motor being dropped into the water off the port side of the yacht. Two men entered. One, obviously the captain, or the one in charge, moved into the bow, while the other one, who appeared to be light-skinned, large and carried what looked like a sub machine gun, went to the stern and operated the outboard engine. After a few seconds firing up, they crossed the distance in less than a minute.

They bumped the side of the PT boat and looked up.

Bill and John looked at each other. It was Bill who moved over to the port side and dropped a rope ladder down to the boat. The one in charge began climbing toward the deck, while the sailor in the back held onto the net. Once the captain was aboard, the second mate started to ascend.

That's when Bill released the ladder and tossed it in the water. The sailor watched helplessly as the PT boat began to drift away.

He raised his arms up to his sides as if to say, "What the hell are you doing?"

Bill just smiled and flipped him off.

"Hey, hey!" the sailor yelled.

Bill smiled, "Fuck you! We'll return you to your boss in a minute. Just sit there, bitch, and you won't get hurt. We told you to come unarmed."

The sailor reached down angrily, grabbed his gun and began to level the M1 rifle towards Bill.

Suddenly, Miguel, running forward from the stern, through the day cabin, appeared on the bridge. He had grabbed his Browning submachine gun off the wall in the day cabin and aimed it over the rail at the sailor He racked it to full auto mode with an audible click! Jack also aimed the port sided twin machine guns on him, which were locked and loaded, while Manolo held the boat steady at the helm. He pushed Kimmi down below the steel shield of the bridge. She looked up at him and glared. "Just for now," whispered Manolo, "If he lowers his gun, you can come up, OK?"

"Best you put that thing down, boy!" was Bill's response.

Reluctantly, the sailor lowered his rifle to the deck and waited ruefully.

Manolo nodded at Kimmi, and she stood up.

The captain boarded the deck of the PT boat and looked around. Standing almost 6'3" and 275 pounds, he looked like he could be a small forward in the NBA or a closing pitcher in Major League Baseball. He appeared to be in his sixties, tanned, had a full head of black hair, a manicured thin black beard and was dressed expensively in tobacco colored designer slacks, tan deck shoes and a rich blue silk shirt, open at the top. He had a small paunch of a belly, which indicated he liked good food and probably good alcohol.

He looked at Bill, who was not holding a weapon, and smiled.

"You must be the Captain Bill whose legend lives up and down the Amazon!" He smiled and put out his hand.

Bill, three feet away, did not smile, nor did he take his hand and, looking him directly in the eye said, "State your business."

The man said, "I am a financier of gold and rare artifacts. My name is Angel Rameriez. My family has many ties to this region and we can not only help finance you, but we have many leads to treasure in this area. With our help, your success would be assured. We wish to help you find the treasure you seek and then, of course, share in the reward."

"Well," began Bill Treese, "What if I was to tell you we didn't need any help and you and your family can just piss off because we've got this covered?"

The smile faded from Angel's face. "Well that would be disastrous for you. Then you will be our enemy and then, you will die."

Bill threw back his head and laughed.

"You! You pissant fucker with your yacht, your Rastas, your half nude bitches!?" You think you can best Bill Treese?"

"How about I release you back to your 'Love Boat' cruise ship and fire a torpedo into it? What say ye to that?"

The look in the man's eye was cold and evil, like a viper. "Just let me get back to my boat. I will deal with you later." He turned to see that his small lifeboat had drifted about 30 feet away, and that his guard was trying to get it started.

He turned back to Bill. "Fuck you, too! I will meet with you again, all in good time!"

Bill smiled and waved. "I am sure you will. How do you want to exit? By your power, or by my power?"

Angel smiled. "Don't trouble yourself. I'm out," as he jumped up and dove head-first into the water and swam toward his life boat.

Bill and the others watched him swim away. John asked, "What do you make of that Bill?" By then, the captain had reached his boat, climbed in and they were making their way back to their yacht.

Bill rubbed his chin. He had been deliberately rude to both of the men from the yacht because he knew they had bad intentions. Years ago, he had allowed men like that into his orbit, against his better judgment. He had barely gotten out with his life, as they tried to commandeer his PT boat, kill him, his crew, and attempted to use the boat to transport drugs and weapons up and down the Amazon. He also knew that he had to put the "fear of God" in them right from the get, or they would try to immediately muscle themselves in. Now he saw it in their eyes, and they would be wary. They, no doubt, would be back, but without the confidence they had shown up with.

Bill looked over at John, "They are not honorable men. They are dangerous. I know that last name 'Rameriez'. The parents were drug runners, slave traders, killers, you name it. They are gone now, but he and his brother are in business. Come to think of it, we may have run into his brother last year in the village. I never made the connection before!" He smiled and sat down on the captain's deck chair at the command console. "I think we need to be wary of them and that they will be watching us dive. They might even try to go in after us. Not today because we have seen each other and they will high-tail it out of here. But they will likely come back and explore the Hole if we are not here, or, like I said, maybe sneak up on us if we are in the water. Who knows?"

CHAPTER THREE
THE TREASURE CHAMBER

BILL, JACK, JOHN, KIMMI, AND MANOLO made preparations for the dive, which would be deep and long. This made decompression stops mandatory. They would be using nitrox, or enriched air diving, meaning the breathing gasses in their tanks would have a higher percentage of oxygen than normal atmospheric air. It was actually known as Enriched Air Nitrox, (EANx), which indicated there was extra oxygen that enriched the mix. This meant the risk of decompression sickness was decreased. This allowed for longer dives at greater depths. This was why Bill had spent almost an hour that morning determining exactly what the mixture of gasses should be for each of them. There was no room for errors in scuba diving, especially considering what they were about to be getting into.

Miguel would stay topside, holding their position and keeping a lookout. The water was relatively warm, so they were all wearing 5mm shortie wet dive suits, except for Bill, who dove in a full 3 mm wet suit. He liked the thinner, but fuller suit.

They each had an emergency pony bottle pack of air, which would give them a few extra minutes of air, if necessary. Bill had placed two tanks with octopus regulators attached on a line going down into the Hole, which would serve as decompression stops. One was at 50 feet and the other at 25 feet.

They assembled on the aft deck of the PT boat, with Bill giving the final instructions.

"We are going down to the wreck that Manolo and I discovered last week, before the storm. I don't know if it will be in the same position as the last time because it may have shifted with the tide and the weather."

"We need to establish 100 percent who she was if we can, and then see what else is down there. If we go inside the hull, below decks, we need to secure a line, so that we have a way out."

"Jack and John are buddies on this dive. Kimmi, Manolo and I are buddies. Stay with your buddy! If anyone gets below 500 pounds of air pressure, let one of us know immediately. This is a situation where the man, or woman, who has the least air, has the priority of the dive. Also, remember if you hear the dive horn, come up as fast as you safely can because Miguel has seen a problem and wants to get us out of the water quickly."

"Ladies and gentlemen, we are not here to push the tables off the charts. We are here to dive safely so we can dive another day. Everybody got that?"

The others all nodded.

"OK," Bill said, "Everybody make a final check of your and your buddies dive gear."

Kimmi thought back to when she and her dad had been certified by PADI (Professional Association of Dive Instructors) instructors, but they were still learning to dive. Their first real complex open water dive together would be off Monastery Beach in Carmel, California. They were in line with other scuba enthusiasts to dive off of Point Lobos, which only allowed 15 teams of two divers per day. Jack had a friend who regularly camped out there the night before, and he was at the head of the line. He would check in as John's dive buddy. Jack, who had the most experience as a diver, would check in as Kimmi's buddy, where he could keep an eye on her, as this was her first dive in Carmel. Fortunately, there were only about 20 divers in line, so they were good to go.

Jack's friend, and his patient, Dave Johnson, walked back in the line to meet John and Kimmi. He was 26, with blond hair and blue eyes. He was well built and lifted weights. He also competed in triathlons. He shook hands with everyone and thanked them for checking in with him and being his buddy. He took a long appreciative look at Kimmi, who was wearing tight workout clothes and, with her long dark hair and pretty Asian features, looked very lovely in the early morning sun. He smiled, "Are you going to be my dive buddy?" he asked innocently.

Kimmi giggled and said, "I'm with my Uncle Jack!" she said, hugging Jack tightly. "You get to buddy up with my dad!" They all laughed.

Dave said, "Well the good news is I brought my 18-foot Zodiac raft, with a big Johnson motor. That way we can get out to the dive site quickly. We're going to dive near the edge of the canyon, but we'll be in the kelp forest, so we will be safe.

Kimmi looked around nervously, "I heard the canyons drop to over 10,000 feet near the shore and they can drag a diver down in the current until he or she runs out of air!"

Dave had been through this with other novice divers. "Yes, that is true," he said, "but the four of us will be diving more or less together, so we will watch each other's back. Jack and I have been on hundreds of dives down here and we've never had an incident. When we launch we will go out to the kelp forests and dive straight down. It goes to about a hundred feet where we are going, but because we would deplete our air quickly at that depth, we will try to stay around 75 feet." He looked around at the blue skies and the calm water, "It should be a great day to dive. Yesterday the water had over 80 feet of visibility." They all nodded. The line started to move, so Dave and John sprinted up to the front of the line to be checked in by the California State ranger.

Dave pulled his boat and trailer to the launch ramp at Whaler's Cove. They loaded their gear aboard and got into their wetsuits. They all helped launch the boat into the water. They moved the boat away from the ramp and held it by a strong rope, while Dave parked his truck. Dave then got into the boat and started the engine with a push button starter, but kept it in neutral. Jack, Kimmi and John climbed aboard. Dave then used an oar to push them away from the shore. Finally, he lowered the engine's propeller into the water, and slowly pulled away from the shore. He began to sail them to a spot near the Pinnacles, or two raised skinny rock-formations, which were off Granite Point.

The dive had been everything Dave said it would be. Kimmi and John had some trouble entering the water because the kelp was all around them, floating on the surface, but Dave had told them to relax and just push it out of the way. At first, Kimmi thought it was just floating by itself, but Dave told her it was actually attached to the ocean floor and grew so tall that the tops just floated on the surface. Dave also showed them how to use their dive knives to cut themselves free, just in case they did become tangled in the kelp. But he discouraged this, as this site was protected as a California state park, and they were not allowed to take anything out of the site, such as shells, rocks, or damage anything on top of or below the surface.

Kimmi was nervous when she entered the water, but Jack helped her move the kelp away and told her to breath into her regulator. She was being bounced around by some of the waves and began to hyperventilate. Jack told her to put her face into the water and look through her mask. She suddenly saw how beautiful and serene it was under the water and calmed down immediately. She could see all the way to the ocean floor, which meant the visibility would be excellent! Her nervousness gave way to the thrill of exploring a new world full of adventure. Her previous diving experiences had been in mostly murky water, off of a beach, with poor visibility. She and her dad had gotten their certifications, but it wasn't really as fun as this looked like it was going to be. Her Uncle Jack had promised to take them to the beautiful waters of Hawaii, where he had dived on wrecks, reefs and in caves off Maui, the Big Island and Oahu.

Because of the coldness of the water, they all wore 7mm full dive suits, with headpieces, to keep their heads warm. Unfortunately, the thicker suits were also more buoyant and forced them to wear more weights around their waist to keep them below the surface.

All four of them gave the "OK" sign, raised their buoyancy control device inflator/deflator hoses up, pressed the button, which would allow the air to escape from the vest, and caused them to slip below the surface. They descended slowly until they were just above the ocean floor, at about 75 feet. John and Kimmi looked around excitedly. There were hundreds of fish, rock formations, plants and the base of the kelp forest, anchored to the sandy bottom. They floated horizontally above the sea floor and began to swim forward. They were near the end of the kelp forest, when Dave gestured to John and Kimmi. He had a white, small slate to write on and he pointed to the area beyond the kelp beds. **"DANGER! Don't go past the kelp or you will be in the canyon!"**

They both nodded and all four turned around and swam back the way they came. Suddenly two small seals came darting out from behind a rock formation. Both Kimmi and John were initially startled because they were the biggest creatures they had seen down there, but relaxed as the seals came closer to them, to satisfy their curiosity. Jack and Dave motioned for Kimmi and John to back away because the seals were protected mammals. All four resumed swimming. Dave and Jack were taking them to a spot that was a little deeper. They swam to a large area that had several big boulders, bordering all around the sandy bottom. They pulled up vertically. Dave tapped their depth gauge. They all realized that they were at 100 feet and were excited. Dave pointed his thumb up, which meant they needed to swim up a little to conserve their air. He looked at everyone's air gauge and, just to make sure, asked them to indicate to him their air level. Using their hands, they flashed out how many hundreds of pounds of air they had left in their scuba tanks. Everyone was good, with John having the least amount of air, but enough left so that they could continue the dive.

The four of them moved forward. Dave looked back to locate his boat's anchor chain. It was about 70 feet away. He planned to swim a little closer to the edge of the kelp forest, just so they could look once again into the abyss, which was the edge of the canyon. That's when he suddenly saw it.

Dave pulled up and went vertical on the water, holding his arms out and waving them frantically. The other three swam up next to him as he pointed to the area just on the other side of the kelp. It was a huge blue whale, not more than twenty feet away! It was swimming slowly, but looking at them with a natural curiosity. Kimmi, shocked, almost started to swim up and away, but Jack grabbed her and shook his head vigorously. He held her as the whale swam slowly past. It was like standing on the ground and watching a huge 18-wheel truck drive past because it was the biggest mammal on earth. Dave thought it had to be at least 80 feet long, (24 m) and probably weighed in at

160 tons. But the fact that it was huge, alive and taking its time swimming past them, was a once-in-a-lifetime event!

After the whale swam out of sight, Dave looked at his dive watch and checked his air. One by one, he asked how much air everyone had left. Everyone was good and had at least 500 pounds of air. He motioned for the rest to follow him back to his anchor chain and they would ascend slowly back to his boat. They had been down almost a full hour and for everyone, it was a fantastic dive. None of them had been that close to a blue whale, or any other whale for that matter, and it would be fun to talk about it over steamed clams, oysters, calamari, and all washed down with a cold Anchor Steam beer on tap at Fisherman's Warf in Monterey!

Kimmi, coming back to reality, smiled and looked over at Manolo. "Baby Whales Really Are Fun," she said to a confused Manolo.

"What?" he asked her.

"Baby Whales Really Are Fun," she repeated with a big smile. "B for buoyancy control devices all checked out, connections made, and functioning properly. W for Weight belts all secure and won't fall off when we hit the water. R for releases all properly working and all have a right-hand release, just in case there is an emergency. A for air, so take a quick couple of puffs of air to make sure you can draw in some air, the valves are all open and that you have your octopus spare breathing air regulator ready for one of us, especially me!" She giggled. "Finally, F is for the final check that all of our gear, including our mask, fins, dive lights, communication systems, are all functioning properly. Don't you do all of that?"

Miguel smiled and nodded, "Yes, but I do it so fast and

automatically, so I didn't know what all of that meant!" He laughed, and it helped to take the tension out of the dive.

Kimmi turned to her other dive buddy, Bill, and asked him, "Do you check your equipment like that, Uncle Bill?"

Bill who was spitting into his mask and rubbing the saliva around the glass to prevent it from fogging, looked at his favorite niece and smiled. "Honey, I've been diving since Vietnam. I always follow a checklist, but it is so automatic that I don't even realize I've been doing it!" He laughed.

"OK, everyone," said Bill. "Let's shove off!"

Bill looked up at Miguel on the bridge and held up a "thumbs up" sign, which on dry land meant he was ready to go, but underwater it meant they needed to ascend up to the surface. Miguel nodded and set his timers accordingly.

Bill, as planned, was the first to jump in the water. He was followed by Kimmi and Manolo. Once they were in the water and moved away, John and Jack jumped in.

Since they all had their buoyancy control vests full of air, the five of them floated on the surface. One by one, they raised the air-tube and pressed the release-button, which emptied the vest full of air and allowed them to sink below the surface into the calm waters.

As they descended into the Blue Hole, Kimmi, John and Jack, thought they had never seen anything like it. The sun shone down hazily, causing the water to seem to ripple and float inside itself, like a drink of whisky, water, and ice cubes in an evening glass. Because the storm had been through, the water was murkier than the other day, and the 100 feet of visibility had been reduced to half of that.

There were thousands of fish. Small, large and everything in-between. There were random jelly fish floating, and, to the concern of John, Jack and Kimmi, several white tipped reef sharks swimming around lazily. As they looked out at the reef, they suddenly saw two scalloped hammerhead sharks swim past them, as if on a mission to find some good food somewhere.

As they descended, they could see multicolored stalactites and stalagmites, which were shaped like icicles left over from the last ice age that helped to shape and form the gigantic Blue Hole.

Following the dive plan, they descended slowly and in order, with the two pairs of buddies dropping 20 feet and then stopping to look around. They were all carrying 15,000 lumens cannister dive lights, that could be dimmed, but which would light up the darkness and turn it into day. They also had lesser power flashlights they could use instead if it was not too dark. Both lights had strobe features, which could be used to alert the divers if there was a potentially dangerous situation on or below the surface.

After a few minutes, with Bill in the lead, they reached the spot where the wreck rested on the shelf.

Shockingly, it was gone!

Immediately, Bill pulled up and signaled the others to come closer. He pointed to the empty shelf, over 100 feet across and gestured emphatically. Since no one except Manolo, knew what had happened, Bill pulled out a pen and wrote on the slate fastened to his arm, *"The ship is gone! The storm must have knocked it off the reef! Let's look around."*

Staying in buddy formation, Jack and John moved ahead over the top of the reef, while Bill, Manolo and Kimmi searched around the front and below, looking for signs of the ship. Bill shone his light to the bottom of the Hole, but could not see the ship. He concluded it had either broken up when it fell off the reef, or it was stuck on another ledge. They couldn't even find the heavy ship's bell with the inscription on it, and it had been buried in the sand and silt on the reef. Bill thought, *it must have been one hell of a storm to knock everything off the reef that had been stuck there for at least 150 years.*

After a while, they all congregated on the shelf where the boat had been. Bill moved toward the rock wall of the Blue Hole, next to the shelf, looking for anything that might help them in their quest.

Bill gathered them around again. He wrote on his board, "Look for an opening, anywhere."

They fanned out, still in buddy formation. It was Kimmi who saw it first. She was following a light tan sediment pattern on the wall which was 10 feet wide at 20 feet above the shelf, went to five feet wide at 10 feet , and then disappeared just above the rock ledge. She swam over with Manolo in tow and Bill, 15 feet away, watching them.

Kimmi began poking around with her dive knife at the base of the wall above the ledge, where she had seen the formation change. Suddenly the rock wall began to cave in and disintegrate before their very eyes! Kimmi tried to pull back, but was being sucked into the cave-in!

Manolo, reached out and tried to grab her, but she was being pulled down and in by the massive cave-in of the rocks, with Manolo being pulled in as well.

Bill shot forward trying to grab them both, but the rocks had become an underwater avalanche and had buried them both!

Bill turned, seeing John and Jack fifty feet away, screamed

through his regulator to come help him. They had heard him and both immediately swam forward to help.

Frantically, they all began pulling rocks away from the cave-in site and hoping to find them unhurt. After the last rock was pulled away, John desperately tried to dive in after his daughter, but Bill stopped him.

Bill shook his head, the much more experienced diver, "I'll get them!" he shouted around his regulator, "You follow! Watch out for more rocks!

They all dove into the chamber looking for their loved ones.

****

Angel Rameriez lay on his back looking up at the ceiling in his yacht. He knew these *gringos* were the ones who had murdered his brother, Andres last year. Andres was looking for the same thing he was — gold. Their parents had both been slave traders in South America of young girls and women. They dealt in cocaine, laundered money, bribed officials and led a life of crime which they had passed on to their children.

Angel and his brother were not particularly close, but since he had died at the hands of these foreigners, then that made it personal. He would be avenged!

He looked down at the young girl who was servicing him orally. He should be paying attention to her and not thinking thoughts of revenge, but here he was.

He reached down and caressed her back. She was 18, full Colombian and beautiful. He reached under her and felt her breasts. It was no use. He couldn't continue — too much on his mind.

He reached over and pulled her chin up to him. He indicated he wanted to kiss her. Smiling, she looked up to him and moved upward and kissed him on the lips. In Spanish, he said, "Thank you lover, but I must leave you now to attend to important matters."

She gave him a pouty look, and he responded by kissing her again.

"Mas tarde," he said, meaning, let's go later, I'm too tired now.

She shrugged and got out of bed. She turned, standing naked before him. Her perfect, dark body shown out to him as if to say, your loss *hombre!* She grabbed her shorts and tee shirt and hurried topside.

Angel sighed, his erection rapidly deflating, as he thought about Bill Treese.

How was he going to neutralize this fucker? he thought to himself.

He had intel that the Blue Hole, which had been explored for years, with no real true treasure discoveries, was worthless. But there was something there which compelled him.

He knew for damn sure Bill Treese would not be here unless he thought there was treasure, and that was enough for him.

Since Bill would not work with him, then he would take all that he could, find out what Bill knew, and kill him in the process.

He got up out of bed, naked and helped himself to the whisky bar in the corner of his stateroom. He selected a *Ron Bacardi de Maestros de Ron, Vintage MMXII* at $2,000 a bottle. He poured the rum into a large snifter. He had had soft mood music playing while he was with the girl. He pressed the volume control on his Bluetooth, and turned the music up a little higher.

He wrapped his white, thick, Egyptian cotton robe around him. He moved to the deck outside his stateroom. Finding a deck chair, he settled in, drinking in the warm, intoxicating rum. He listened to the Hawaiian string music, with the male singer singing a soft ancient tune, and tried to relax.

His brother had missed his chance, he thought as he looked at the large, full moon over the ocean, wrapped up in a billion stars.

He would not.

****

Bill Treese, Jack and John dove into the hole Kimmi had found, which had pulled her and Manolo in with them.

They dove down twenty-five feet and found Kimmi and Manolo sitting at the bottom of a cave. They swam up to them, with Bill gesturing emphatically.

"Are you both all right?"

They both nodded their heads.

"What happened?" Jack asked around his regulator. He and John had caught up to Bill, who was hovering next to Kimmi and Manolo.

Kimmi answered, " It looks like a cave-in to the opening we are looking for! The rocks dragged us down!"

Bill, still shaken up by the unexpected cave-in, nonetheless, shown his powerful light around them. The silt which had been swirling around them since the rock cave-in had begun to settle.

He shined the light up to the top that they had fallen through, then around to the walls they were surrounded by. They were about 25 feet below the ledge that had caved in. He suddenly realized they were inside the walls of the ledge.

Bill was shining his light all around him, then up and down the walls. Trying to get his bearings, he suddenly realized that the wall he was looking at was the one that was part of the wall that formed the side wall of the Hole. He turned to look behind him at the opposite wall. It extended back about 20 feet more. They were actually in a hole within the Blue Hole. He could see that there was what appeared to be a small passageway in that direction. He motioned for Jack to follow him and be his buddy.

The others watched them, waiting on the sandy floor of the new hole they were in.

Bill and Jack approached the passageway, but after about ten feet they came to a dead end. Bill looked at Jack and shrugged.

"What about above us?" Jack said around his regulator.

They both tried to look upward, but the first stage of their regulators would not allow them to elevate their heads very far. But being experienced divers, they did the next best thing – they both rolled onto their backs while hovering above the sea floor and Bill shone his light upward expecting to see a low ceiling and not much more.

What they saw took their breath away. The light shone upward through what looked like an endless passage.

Bill motioned for Jack to get the others. Jack pulled out his dive light and swam over to their dive team. John, Kimmi and Manolo all followed Jack to where Bill was waiting.

On Bill's signal, they all let a little bit of air out of their buoyancy vests, which helped them to rise slowly in the tunnel, which was about 12 feet wide and shaped like a perfectly formed cylinder.

Bill was the first to pop his head out of the water. He realized he was now in some type of cavern. It was dark, and he shown his light around to see that they had emerged into a cave. He looked down at the others who were just below him; he signaled for them to come up by making a fist with his thumb pointed in the air.

There was enough room and they all broke the surface of the water together. Floating, Bill took his regulator out of his mouth. "It's a cave. And it's dry. Go figure!" He sniffed the air, and while it was musty, cold and wet, it seemed to be coming from somewhere.

Gripping the edge of the cave floor, he pulled himself up and wiggled onto dry land. While on one knee, he pulled off his dive mask and buoyancy control device. He dropped his weight belt and kicked off his fins. "Wait here for a second," he told the others. He walked carefully forward and saw that the cave extended back and went another 20 feet, before it made a sharp turn to the left. He touched the walls, which seemed to be made of either hardened lava or some type of limestone.

He returned to the others and said, "Let's leave our gear here and go check this out!"

John, Kimmi, Manolo and Jack all exited the water and dropped their gear next to Bill's.

They followed Bill, as his dive light lit up the cave. They got to the left turn, and carefully Bill looked around it. He shone his light down and there looked to be another turn, but this time to the right. He motioned for the others to follow. The hallway was about 30 feet long. They got to the end, once again, Bill looked around carefully. He found himself looking into a large room which was dark and cold. He used his dive light and what he saw, completely took his breath away.

He stepped in the room and motioned for the others to follow him. As they entered the room, they saw what Bill was shining his light on — a giant pile of gold lay stacked up next to one wall.

Kimmi was the first to speak, "Oh my Lord!"

Jack said, "This is incredible!"

John, a grin spread from ear to ear said, "Now this is archaeology!"

Manolo didn't say anything. He had never seen anything like this in his life.

Bill said, "Go ahead and take your lights out and let's explore this!"

His dive computer on his wrist suddenly pinged twice. It was a signal from Miguel on the PT boat asking if they were OK because they had been down longer than expected. Bill shot a quick message that they were fine, with plenty of air and that they had found something.

Bill looked up to see the ceiling above them, was approximately 20 feet high. Strangely enough, air was coming from somewhere.

He looked at the pile of gold. It was approximately 20 feet wide by 20 feet long and piled up about four feet high. They all moved over to get a closer look. There were hundreds of gold cups, chains, crosses, coins, medallions and solid gold bars. They saw gold ceremonial swords, daggers, fine jewelry and small statues. The enormity of the treasure was staggering. There was also an ornate bed next to the gold, and several steel cutlasses stacked up next to it, which looked like the type of sword a pirate would use. In front, and to the side of the gold, were six sea chests, all with their lids closed. They likely contained more valuables. There were two old fashioned flintlock pistols on the night stand, next to the bed.

Above the bed, was a large oil painting of a pirate, dressed like a swashbuckler of the 19th Century, in black pants tucked into black sea boots, with a rich white shirt, red vest and a red military jacket, adorned with gold braids and buttons. The man stood with his hands on his hips, his jacket pulled back. He had a long black beard and wore a black pirate style hat on his head. He wore a heavy black belt around his waist, with a long sword dangling down on the left, and two flintlock pistols were stuck in the front of his belt, crossing each other, pointing down. He had an expression of one who had mastered his fate and enjoyed his life.

"This room reminds me of The Pirates of the Caribbean Ride at Disneyland!" exclaimed Kimmi. "How did it all get down here?"

"Good question," said Bill. "We know they didn't swim all of this stuff in here. There must be another entrance somewhere that leads to this cave, and whoever owns or owned this stuff brought it here for safekeeping.

They all had taken out their dive lights and everyone started looking around.

Jack went over to look at the pistols, which looked like

they were from the 1700s. He was a gun aficionado, and he loved antique weapons. He picked one of them up. It was a German flintlock pistol with ornate cast brass mounts, which were gold gilded. It was a little rusty, but looked like it could fire, if given the proper care. It was a beautiful gun, with ornate carvings along the steel barrel. He turned it over in his hand and saw a name inscribed on the wooden handle.

Jack said, "Has anyone ever heard of Lester Smith?" he asked. They all shook their heads. John put down the gold cross he had been studying and walked over to Jack. "May I see it?" he asked.

Jack nodded, "But be careful because I don't know if it is loaded or how it could even fire." Pointing the barrel towards the ground, he handed the gun over to John, who studied it carefully. He looked up at Jack, "Does the other gun over there have the same name inscribed on it?" he asked.

Carefully, Jack picked up the other gun. Turning it over in his hand, he realized it matched the gun John was holding. He looked for the inscription on the handle. "Yes, it is the same name!" he said excitedly.

Bill walked over and looked at the guns they were holding. Well, since there are no other names that we have seen so far, then we must assume that this is the treasure of Mr. Lester Smith, whoever he is — or was." Bill looked up at the oil painting of the pirate, "Maybe that was him," he said pointing up.

Both John and Jack nodded in agreement.

Kimmi and Manolo wandered over. "What is the bed like?" she asked.

It was a large wooden four-poster bed, with heavy drapes

on all four sides. There was a large, ornately carved headboard, with what looked to be a three masted sailing ship from the 1700s on it. The wood looked like teak, which would explain why it had survived the dampness of the cave. The drapes were rotted and smelled moldy, likely from when dampness hit the chamber. The mattress had not fared as well and it had come apart, leaving piles of feathers on the floor. The blankets were also rotted.

John spoke up, "The bed frame is likely teak wood, which is why it is still intact. The curtains around the bed were for warmth because it was likely really cold down here at certain times of the year. But who really knows how much he or they stayed?"

They all decided to go back to look at the treasure. "Wow," said Jack, "Now what do we do with it?"

Bill spoke up, "For the time being, nothing. If we discovered a few gold bars or some coins, that would be one thing, but we have unearthed a treasure that is probably in the hundreds of millions of dollars, maybe even in the billions. So we need to sit tight on it, go back up, plug the opening in the ledge and return to the ship. We know how to get back down here. I doubt anyone has been here for the past two centuries, so I don't think it is going anywhere. I want John and I to do some research on the name of Lester Smith and see if we can piece this together. We will dive here again in the morning. Let's get back to the boat."

He checked his dive tables. He calculated they were approximately 85 feet underwater. "We will need to take two five-minute decompression stops on the way up, one at 50 feet and one at 25 feet. There are tanks set up at those levels, if you need more air. Everyone check their air when we get back to the entrance. If anyone has less than 500 pounds of air, you need to buddy up with me because I have a lot left in my tank. Let's get going!"

They all turned and followed Bill back to the opening, that would lead them into the water and to the Blue Hole.

CHAPTER FOUR

CAPTAIN LESTER SMITH AND THE UNION ARMY

CAPTAIN LESTER SMITH WOKE UP EARLY in his cabin and stretched. He climbed out of his bunk and reached around in the darkness looking for his pants, boots and shirt. After a few minutes, he dressed and left his cabin through the water tight hatch, ducking low because of his height. He went into the galley and made a large pot of coffee. He sat down at the small table and thought about his day ahead.

Today was a working day on his island named Trinity. Instead of his usual pirate garb, he wore heavy denim blue jeans, a short-sleeved, red plaid cotton shirt and heavy-duty work boots.

He, his first mate Trinidad and his other five sailors, were going to search the island, looking for the treasure chamber his great grandpa had described in his diary. While they were all in on the search, he would only be showing the book to Trinidad. While he trusted his men, anyone can get gold fever and make a lethal mistake, which would cost lives. So, he took precautions.

He looked at his watch. Trinidad would be here any minute to look at his great grandpa's diary, which was large, thick, and over 150 years old. Most of it was still intact; he kept it in a teak chest, which was lined with cedar wood, under his bunk, in a larger metal sea chest, which he kept locked at all times.

At that moment, he heard heavy footsteps on the deck of his boat, coming close to the ladder. The boat was kept well-hidden from the open ocean on their island of Trinity. There was a natural bay, which led inland. It appeared from the outside, that the bay ended at a large, steep cliff, which soared up over 800 feet, and was impossible to climb. However, what was not seen, was a cave which existed behind a curtain of vines and tropical trees. The cave's opening was fairly small and existed at a right angle to the waterway, making it impossible to see, and even if someone should happen to sail up the bay, they would be stopped by the jungle carpet. In addition, Captain Lester always had one or two sentries on duty.

The sailors lived in small huts, which were in a clearing, also behind the cave. They had running water from the mountains, grew some simple crops, and had a small warehouse, partially underground, made of concrete bricks and slate, which was always cool inside, no matter what the temperature was outside. Here they kept their beer, wine and rum. They also hung meat inside to cure.

This was all started by Captain Lester's parents, who were true pirates and drug runners. They had spent their lives robbing merchants, selling drugs, alcohol and whatever they could on the black market. When Captain Lester, who never fully embraced being a pirate, but was doing what he was taught to survive, was

20 years old, both of his parents were killed by the Jamaican Navy in a fierce battle at sea.

Fortunately, Lester was staying with his grandpa and grandma in Kingston, Jamaica at the time. He had been wounded in a battle a month before and was sent home to recover.

His grandparents were honest people, who worked as teachers and never went in for the dangerous lifestyle. For whatever reason, their son, Captain Lester's father, and his wife did.

There was a knock on the top of the ladder. "Ahoy, Captain," came the familiar voice of his friend, Trinidad, *"Entre, ya?!*

"Ya, *mon.* Please do. Thank you for being on time!"

Trinidad climbed down the ladder. Lester stood up and they embraced. They were best friends and treated each other with respect and love.

"Coffee, Trinidad?"

"Yes, indeed, thank you!"

Lester smiled as he poured Trinidad a large cup of his coffee, which was pure Jamaica Blue Mountain coffee. They had picked up several cases when they last hit port. They had to be careful. They had never committed any crimes on their native land of Jamaica, but many crimes at sea.

Technically, they were not wanted men at home, but merchant marines of other countries might not feel so inclined. In fact, had they ever been caught by sea merchants, they would likely just be hung and dumped over the side and their boat sunk.

After they had passed a few pleasantries, they got down to business.

"I have been looking forward to seeing your great grandpa's

diary all night," Trinidad said excitedly.

Lester smiled. "Ya. I will show you the things which are specific to this adventure, but not the whole diary. There are many personal details about mi family, which need to stay with us, but I will tell you. *Yu done know,* (You understand)?"

"*Irie, mon.*"

Lester began, "*Mi* great grandpa, he was a *stinga,* the girls all loved him back in the day. He was a *stulla lover.* That's why he left Jamaica. He was hot and, when he was eighteen, he got *mi* great grandma pregnant. But he had no job, no way to support her.

"Her father said he was a *waste man,* a useless person. But he had done good in school and one of his teachers knew a professor at Oxford in England. He knew mi great grandpa was very smart and that if he got an education, he would be able to provide for his girl and new baby.

"He went to the girl's father and told him about the offer to go to England and study at Oxford. No *mon* from our island went there. The father was going to have him arrested and flogged to death. But the girl begged her father to spare him and hear his plan.

"Mi great grandpa was pretty smart. He went to the town banker and said he was going to study finance and trade at Oxford. He asked the banker if he could have a job when he returned in four years. The banker said yes. He also borrowed some money for the education, even though he had none collateral. But the banker believed in him and gave him the money.

"He took his plan to her father and he said, he would bless them under these conditions:

He had to marry the girl, he had to come back and work for the father for 10 years, doing labor if he failed at his studies, that he had to put up a money bond, if he failed and if he did not return, his parent's lands would be held in forfeit.

"He agreed to the terms. He was in England when his son, mi grandpa was born. He sailed back to Jamaica in four years, after graduating at the top of the class, to be reunited with his wife and son. They lived with her parents for one year while he worked at the bank. Because of what he learned, the bank, which was small, started making loans to other islands and, after a decade, was making loans to the Americans. He was able to do *big tings, mon,* (Monetary success)."

"Dat shot!" replied Trinidad, "Making lots of *cheddar!* Then what?"

"That's when the Civil War broke out and the Union Army couldn't get the Confederates out of Charleston Harbor. So, they came looking for an army man and that was mi great grandpa."

"Trinidad asked, "What was he name, *mon?*""

Lester smiled, "Mr. Lester Smith, Esquire. He also got a degree in law from Oxford, while he was there!"

Trinidad was silent for a minute, then he spoke up, "Your namesake, Captain?"

"Ya, mon."

"That's maad, mon!"

Lester smiled. He got up and went into his cabin. He retrieved the diary and brought it back to the table. He set it down and picked up the two empty cups of coffee. There would be no food or drink at the table, as he valued this book with his life.

"Remember, *mon,*" Lester said, "he was educated at Oxford University in England. He writes like an educated man. Not as much like us," he added.

They both gazed at it with wonder. It was the size of a modern-day Bible, but not as thick. The black leather cover was cracked and faded. Lester had placed a silk ribbon attached to the cover on a certain page. Carefully, he opened it. The writing was spidery and thin, but looked eloquent. It was as though Lester's great grandpa had put a lot of time, love and energy into the book, hoping future generations would be educated and warned about the events of the day, and possibly events which would come in the future.

Captain Lester Smith began to read:

"Diary entry, April, 20, 1863, going forward:

The Americans arrived in Kingston. There were two of them, who sailed over on a U.S. Warship. Both white men. One was Lieutenant Jones and the other was Captain Barnes.

Our intelligence people had had some conversations and whisperings that they wanted to hire our soldiers, to take out the Confederates, who were stationed at Fort Sumpter. Their plan was to pin the Confederates, between the fort and the sea, with our people attacking them from the sea. They would then be in a cross-fire from the Union and then from us.

I do not trust these blue devils. They have great blue uniforms, medals of war on their lapels, big ranks and insignias, but they lie. Several times they say one thing, then the other contradicts them, by saying something else. They make several references to how they like to free the Negros, and wasn't it nice that we, on our island, were freedmen. I explained to them we were not freedmen, but had always been free on our island. They laughed and said, that is because no white man would live in this hot place. Then they would enslave you because you are Negros.

I took this as an insult. I asked why they were at war with their own countrymen and they say, it is because of your people.

Jamaicans? I asked, knowing what they really meant.

No, they say because of the Negros! We want to free them.

Why, I ask?

Because slavery is bad.

What will you do with them if you win, I ask.

They stopped talking after that. Then they say, how much for your soldiers to come help us?

I say how many of my men do you want? How many will die in your service?

They didn't like my questions.

We need five hundred soldiers. We guarantee their safety. We will pay you one thousand in gold bars.

I smile. Two dollars for a life? I ask. I value a life at one thousand dollars, paid in advance.

They both laughed at me.

I did not laugh. I stared at them. I said, for five hundred

thousand in gold bar, you get 500 men, plus five ships to carry them on. There will be a crew on each ship, who will fire at the Confederates with cannons. The soldiers will come over in boats and attack the Confederates. It will be over in one week. You cannot guarantee my men's safety because this is war. I believe less than half my men will return to our Island, and those that do will never be the same again. But they would do it for their families. For the money.

The captain and the lieutenant said they would get back to me and left. Without shaking my hand. I knew they saw my skin color as being dirty.

The next morning, I received a communication. They would agree to my terms and asked how soon we could leave. I sent word, I demanded the half the money immediately and the other half when we were assembled and ready to leave the docks.

Reluctantly they agreed. The next day, 250,000 in gold bars was delivered to my office, which I deposited this with the banker. He was instructed to pay the soldiers and their families, 50 percent and the ship companies, captains and crew 25 percent. We keep 25 percent. Once we get the final payment in one week after assembling the crew and the soldiers, the final 250,000 would be distributed in the same way.

In one week, we were all assembled at the docks. It was a mighty flotilla of an army, ready to go to war. All soldiers had been explained the risks and all had agreed. The money was more than they would make in many years as laborers and would help their families.

The morning held blue skies and there was a good wind blowing to take us out to sea. The captain and the lieutenant arrived, smiling and waving at the troops, who waved back and cheered lustily, waiting to shove off. It was a great day for everyone!

I greeted them formally. They would not shake my hand, so I did not offer it. After a few nice words, they pulled me aside and said there was a problem with the rest of the money. We would be paid the rest when we reached Charleston. He said a rider was coming from Washington to bring us the money.

I smiled at them.

The captain said I had half the money and could wait.

I smiled again. I turned away and shouted to the soldiers and to the captains of the ships one by one. Please dismount we are not being paid.

Yells and shouts came from the men. Angrily they began coming off the gangplanks to the docks. Several walked up to the two soldiers and started screaming at them.

They backed up. What are you doing they asked?

I said we are done. We are keeping the money you have paid us so far and canceling the attack.

NO! they said. You cannot do that!

I am doing that, I said. Unless you produce the rest of the money right now as agreed.

They both started to curse me and began to draw

their pistoles, but 20 of my men jumped them and started to hit them!

They yelled Stop, Stop, so I shouted an order and my men backed off. I grabbed a cutlass from one of my men, and going to the captain laying on the deck, I held the tip to his chest and yelled, Produce the money or I will run you through!

His lieutenant started to jump up and come after me, but one of my men kicked him in the head and he dropped back to the deck. Blood came out of his mouth and I was happy.

Captain Barnes held up his hands. Don't run me through. I will bring you the money tomorrow. But then you will sail with us back to Charleston. If the soldiers do not attack, then we will hang you from our yardarms in front of your countrymen and our boats will sink your boats.

I did not smile at him because I knew that was what they were really planning to do to me.

They were going to pay us, but then use our soldiers to do their bidding. But because, I knew, President Lincoln had not authorized this, they were going to say I led an attack on the Union, but because we were stupid Negros, we attacked the Confederates by mistake. They would then look blameless. The Confederates would be crushed, most of my men would be dead, and I would be hanged for treason for leading these rebels from Jamaica.

I agreed with him. Be here in the morning and I will sail with you, said I.

I went to our admiral. I told him everything, including the details of the financial deals. I asked him for a commission to make it real to the Americans. He appointed me as a captain and made the arrangements. He agreed to everything, including to follow the American vessel I would be on. They would then make the decision to attack the Confederates or rescue me and return home. I told them if I appeared on deck in shackles, they would know and then they could attack the vessel. We would then return to Jamaica, with their money and all of us safe.

The next morning, the Union soldiers brought the gold in a chest to the docks. Our banker took the money. I was escorted up the gangplank onto the U.S. vessel. Once onboard, they knocked me unconscious and I was placed in chains below deck.

On the second day, I asked for some water and food. They laughed and said camels like me didn't need food and water. We could store it in our humps. They laughed at me. I had to sleep in my own urine.

By the next day, they threw water on me because I stank in my own waste. They said they were nearing the U.S. and would be taking me to the fort and hanging me for treason.

I asked them, appearing weak and lifeless, if I could speak to the captain or the lieutenant.

After a time, the captain came down to my brig. What do you want boy, he said.

Nothing sir, I said with all the humility and

sadness I could muster. Are my men in position to battle soon, sir?

Yes, he said. In 2 hours. Are they in sight? No, he said they are ahead of us.

Captain, can you please execute me now? On deck? I do not wish to watch this.

Please, I added.

He smiled at me and that bastard, he ran up on deck and returned with two of his guards.

He said bring this fucker up on deck. Leave the chains on! We are going to hang his ass by the neck until he is dead!

They grabbed me and, I am sure holding their noses, dragged me to the deck.

The sun blinded me, but I hoped my Navy was behind me.

They brought me up to the yardarms and were about to hoist me up and throw a rope around my neck. I looked around in the blinding light.

Captain! Captain! I yelled.

What?" came his reply.

I am a Christian, captain, although I may not look like it to you. Can someone please say a prayer over my soul before I die? It would mean something to me before I meet my Lord Thy God!

The captain turned around and faced the sea. He sighed heavily, as if he just wanted to get on with my hanging. It was mid-morning and the sun came shining down. He must have been torn between being a savage soldier and being a Godly man, which was probably how he was raised by God-fearing, Christian parents. Who knows what had happened to him to make him leave his faith.

Slowly, the captain turned and nodded his head twice. "Fuck head," I heard him mutter under his breath.

Bring up the cook! he shouted, who was probably the religious leader onboard.

I prayed he would take his time, but the cook came up on deck immediately. He started to pray out loud, LORD! Hear our prayer. Bless this poor devil and commit him whatever mercy you can spare his bastardly hide, Lord! Amen!

They started to hoist me up the yardarms after throwing a rope around my neck. I thought it was all over. I began to say my own prayers to my Lord, the Almighty God and Jesus, for my eternal soul.

Then, suddenly, the cannons rang out from my mates on the other vessels, who had been following us. Not less than four, three masted vessels were now firing on us. The sailors released me as I fell to the deck. They had panicked, and the men all manned their guns and began to fire back at my ships and my mates.

My hands were bound behind me, so I was able to lay on my back, pull up my feet and get them in front of me. I threw the noose off and dove headfirst into the ocean, swimming like a madman. I reached the first boat of my flotilla and grabbed the rat line. I climbed up and reached the deck. A sailor rushed over to me and pulled me up and below decks as the firing raged. We were four and they were one.

We sank their vessel in flames and glory, then turned around and all our boats headed back to Jamaica.

We kept their money. We would have honored our agreements with them, but they were scoundrels and would have let our men die and kept our money.

They had no love for our people. So, we became pirates because now there was a price on our heads. We attacked Union ships, merchant ships, foreign ships that we knew were going to help the Union Army. They won the Civil War eventually, of course. But we continued our pirating as they tried to rebuild their nation.

We made a fortune. There was so much gold, we had to find a safe place to store it because by that tyme there was a huge price on our heads. We took a lot of the gold out and gave it to the government and the people of Jamaica. But there was so much that we needed to keep it safe. It would keep our families wealthy for many generations to come.

We went to our island. We found a break in the rocks. We found a natural rock, maybe a lava tube, passageway that led to a cavern. It was under the ocean away from the island. We stored it all there. We kept pirating, until we became too old. I left the island forever one day and settled in Kingston.

Both Lester and Trinidad were silent for a minute.

"Was that the end of the diary?" asked Trinidad.

"No, there is a lot more talk about his piratin' days and when he had one of his ships shot out and sunk from under him. Somewhere around our island, but they never found it, ya. Also, stories that involves his life with his wife and children, and also what he did after he returned to Jamaica. Lots of personal things, ya. His possessions, his famous personal swords he had made, some lost. But that is what I wanted to read you, so you would know where I was comin' from, *mon.*

"He was a good man, then?" asked Trinidad.

"Ya, *mon*, he was *Gaza!* He stood his ground! Killed those bad men!

"What about the rest of the gold? Do you thing he took it all with him?"

"No, there is another passage that says he took all that he and his family needed, sealed up the entrance to the tunnel, and left this diary with the clues on where to find it. But he didn't make it too easy because if the diary was lost, they would know where to look. His grandson, mi, daddy, took *I and I* to the island with mi mum. That was their port, until they died. They looked for the cave for years, as have I."

"How did you come to have his name?"

"They say I looked like him when I was born. So that's how. Later I grew big like him and was *creng!* I lifted weights all day long. I wanted to play rugby like you! Later, I began to fight, and those men at the bars in Kingston would bet on me. I made money fighting those weak bastards, so they paid me. More and more, I demanded from them. Along with piratin' on those boats, until mi parents wanted me on board. That was until I got hurt and had to return to Jamaica. Mi grandpa and mi grandma looked after me. They kept me long after I was able to go back, because they loved mi and didn't want mi to return to that life. Then mi ma and pa got killed and that ended it, ya. Mi grandparents grieved for a while, but knew that was their son's destiny, so they put their faith in mi. I'm still a pirate, but with a plan to end this life and do something better, ya.

"You still do *big tings,* me *Bredda!*

"Ya, *mon.* Let's work together! Let's go find the gold!"

****

All that night after the dive, Bill and John researched the name Captain Lester Smith on the internet. What they came up with was that there were two Captain Lester Smiths from Jamaica. One lived during the American Civil War and had a situation where he was supposed to help the Union Army defeat the Confederate Army, but because of some kind of swindle, wound up abandoning the Unionists and leaving them to the savages of the war.

The second entry was vague and mentioned a Captain Lester Smith, also known as Blackbeard, who attacked merchant ships at sea and relieved them of their cash and cargo.

They all discussed their findings over supper and drinks. Manolo made an excellent fish stew with plenty of beans, vegetables, red potatoes and some shrimp. He had also cooked some local corn-on-the-cob, he had picked up in town when they went to the airport to pick up John, Jack and Kimmiko.

John spoke up, "It would seem we have maybe two pirates, over a hundred years apart, but maybe after the same objective!"

Jack chimed in, "If they were related, the younger one should know of the older one and maybe aspired to be like him. Right?"

Kimmi, excited by the speculation, and the fact that she had just graduated from the School of Archaeology from U.C. Berkeley, had a few ideas of her own. She said, "So let's look at this from a historical perspective. What if the first Captain Lester was a Civil War disturber, who became an unexpected plunderer due to the Unionists, who were dishonest. Wouldn't he pass that down to his children and grandchildren? What would they do? Follow in his footsteps? It sounds like he was an unwilling participant in a bad situation? Wouldn't he want his offspring to follow a straighter path? This new Captain Lester sounds like a true pirate, who makes his money off profiteering from innocent but maybe stupid tourists, who are in the wrong place at the wrong time. Maybe we can find him and enlighten him on a better path?"

They were all silent for a minute. Bill spoke up, "My sweet niece has hit the nail on the head, so to speak. If we find him and he doesn't try to kill us, we can ask him some of those questions. But the reality is he likely pirating for a reason? Does he need the money, or does he just enjoy it? So, who knows?" They all went back to their dinner.

Bill had pulled out some rare Cabernet Sauvignon and Chardonnay wine he had been saving. He let them all drink as much as they wanted, because they were safe for the moment, but once they made progress on the treasure, then there would likely be much more difficulties going forward.

He himself didn't drink that night. He was too deep in thought and wanted to maintain a clear head.

The next morning, they all assembled on the deck at 0900 hours. Manolo had made breakfast burritos of ham, egg and cheese. There was coffee and orange juice. Since they were going to dive, they couldn't eat a lot. Miguel expertly drove the boat to the edge of the Blue Hole. Bill had told him to keep an eye out for the party boat and the guys they had encountered. Bill hoped he had scared them away, but he doubted it. Everyone knew this Blue Hole had been explored a thousand times and there was, supposedly, no treasure to be found, but people were always hopeful and, as he thought, unpredictable.

Jack, John, Kimmi, Manolo and Bill were going to descend as before, but they were going to look for the tunnel at the other end of the treasure chamber, which would lead them to dry land. They had cameras to record the treasure in the cave. John and Kimmiko were going to try to catalogue as much of the treasure as they could. Kimmi's anthropology studies at U.C. Berkeley were coming in handy. She had learned a lot there, but working alongside her dad was proving to be a real joy. Bill had asked Manolo to use his locksmith skills to try and open the treasure chests which they had seen the day before. The thought was, that since all of the gold was just laying out in the open, then what could be locked away in the treasure chests? They were all excited to find out.

They cast off and wound up in the treasure chamber in about 20 minutes.

Everybody took off their scuba gear and left it at the entrance to the cave. They had brought electric, waterproof lanterns with them, so they did not have to rely on their scuba lights as much. They could also stay down a little longer, but because they were below sea level, they would still have to make decompression stops, when returning to the PT boat, to avoid the bends.

Jack and Bill were going to go up and explore if there was a way down here from some topside island.

Once everyone was settled into the treasure chamber, Bill and Jack set off looking for the source of the cave. Touching the sides of the cavern, they eventually found a way out and up. It was dry and the cavern was easily ascended.

The tunnel's walls were coarse and thick. They knew they were under water, but having left their scuba gear back at the entrance to the treasure cave, they did not know how deep they actually were. They believed that they were getting shallower because they were steadily moving up hill. They could also smell fresh air coming from whatever was in front of them

Suddenly, as they rounded a bend in the tunnel, they could see daylight. The tunnel ended abruptly at a rock wall. There was only a small slit of light coming from the side of what looked like an ancient doorway. Bill motioned Jack to stay behind him. He peeked through the crack and could see the ocean!

"Jack," he whispered, "how far do you think we walked from the treasure cave?"

Jack shrugged, "Maybe a mile or two?"

"Yeah. That's what I was thinking."

"Why?" asked Jack.

"Well, there are about 20 islands near the Blue Hole. I was trying to figure out which one it might be. But having said that, I don't want to tip our hand, otherwise the hunt for this treasure would take an ugly turn."

"Everybody around here knows there is no treasure down there because people have been diving here for years, but no one found what we found!"

"Beginners luck!" said Jack.

Bill looked out as much as he could through the crack. He could see some small huts and a rock hill to his left, but that was it. There was some type of vegetation over the crack, like vines or something. There was no door handle, or frame. Just what looked like a rock wall. He wasn't sure how they would get through it. Maybe a sledge hammer or dynamite.

Bill turned to Jack. "It is pretty much sealed and we need to leave it that way, at least for now. There are huts and probably people out there. But it is obvious that no one has passed through this door for at least a couple of centuries, so let's leave it at that."

"Can I look?" asked Jack.

Bill moved back so Jack could look out. "Yeah, there are a couple of huts and the ocean, but not much else. We kind of backdoored this whole thing, didn't we?" said Jack.

Bill nodded and looked through the crack one more time.

They turned to go back to the treasure chamber.

Manolo had worked his magic on five of the treasure chests. They had contained more gold bars and religious artifacts. John and Kimmi had been going over the gold artifacts and were trying to identify their significance in history.

Manolo was having trouble with the final chest. No matter what he tried, the lock would not open up. He was getting frustrated. Just then, Bill and Jack returned from their trip to the other end of the cave.

"Hi guys," Bill said. "How is it going?"

John spoke up, "There is so much treasure here, it would take months to sort it all out. Identifying it is one thing, but trying to figure out where it came from is really frustrating."

"Yes," Kimmi chimed in, "it's all gold, but there are cups, swords, daggers, crosses, chains! There is so much to figure out."

"Sure," said Bill, "you could melt it all down and just keep the gold, but who wants to destroy rare artifacts that are over 200 years old? Many of these objects could probably be traced back to the time of Christ!"

Kimmi asked Bill, "Did you find the end of the tunnel?"

"Yes," said Bill, "it ended at some small village. There were no people present, so we couldn't tell if it was abandoned or not. There was only a small crack that we could look through. I could see the ocean, a couple of huts and some kind of hill. Plus, there was vegetation growing all over it. If it was an entrance to the treasure chamber, it has been sealed for a very long time, centuries even!"

"Oh wow!" Kimmi said.

"Got it!" Manolo cried when the lock on the final sea chest popped open.

Everybody came over and looked inside, expecting to see more of the gold bars and coins, like the other chests held. There was a heavy gold blanket over the top of whatever was inside and on top, a single piece of parchment paper directly in the center with thin spidery writing on it in black ink.

They all looked at each other.

It was John, the archaeologist who picked it up and read it out loud.

January 31, 1888.

If you are reading this note then I am dead and you will soon join me. There is nothing but death in this chamber and on this island. Look inside, my friend, and behold your future.

Captain Lester Smith, Esq.

The hairs on the back of John's neck stood on end. He placed the note back onto the gold blanket and looked around at the others.

"Well that was charming," said John.

Bill spoke up, "What the hell. We've already been cursed by the first treasure we found. We can't die more than once!"

Bill got down on his knees, placed the note on the floor and removed the gold blanket. They all moved forward and looked inside.

There were three heavy hand daggers, each almost two feet long, with gold handles, richly adorned with jewels, pearls and what appeared to be abalone shell. It was obvious that these were the same styled daggers that he and Manolo had found on the sunken ship!

Just like the other ones, the sheaths covering the blades were also made of thick gold and richly adorned. Knowing what he would find, Bill drew out the blades one by one and set them on the gold blanket, that had covered them for centuries.

They all had the same carvings on the steel as the other daggers.

John was the first to speak, "So we now have two matching

sets of the same daggers, one found on a wrecked ship and one found here in the treasure cave." He shrugged, "Maybe they're really steak knives and they gave them out as door prizes, you know, if you like opened an account at a Jamaican bank," he said, trying to be funny.

Jack picked one of them up. "It's ok, it says 'made in Hong Kong' on it." He smiled.

Bill was rubbing his chin thoughtfully. "Since we know, or think, that this is the cave of Captain Lester Smith, and there are matching daggers on the sunken ship, is it too far of a stretch to think that maybe the ship was also his?"

The others nodded in agreement.

"When we get back to the PT boat, let's try to find out what kind of ship or ships he sailed on during his pirating days," said Bill. "I'm going to put these swords in a waterproof bag and bring them up. I want to compare them all side by side and see if I can match the inscriptions on the blades."

Jack asked, "How are we with the dive tables? We've been down here awhile and you and I walked up basically to sea level."

Bill took a minute to check his dive watch. He punched in a few numbers and then waited a minute. He looked back at his watch. "We're OK," he said. "Same as before. Two decompression stops on the way back up to the boat. I'm going to signal Miguel that we will be starting our ascent."

CHAPTER FIVE

THE ATTACK

ANGEL RAMERIEZ HAD TAKEN HIS YACHT BACK to his home port. He had offloaded the party men and women and brought onboard his private team of mercenary soldiers. There were six of them, including his first mate. They were all trained in Underwater Demolition Technology, or UDT, as taught to Navy Seals. They all had automatic weapons, handguns and other weapons for both above ground and below water combat.

His yacht was fast. It would go 70 miles per hour and get back to the Blue Hole in record time. Once they got near the dive site, they would stop short and survey the situation to see if the PT boat was still there, or if they had left.

He wasn't planning on attacking them directly on the surface; the PT boat had too much firepower for that. But if they were diving and possibly bringing up treasure, then they would try to sneak up on them, board them and kill them.

Their other option was to wait for them to dive and then

follow them into the Blue Hole and see if they had discovered treasure after all. If so, they could potentially eliminate them. He was at the helm of his boat, while the men were below deck, some sleeping, some playing cards or reading. He would navigate until midnight and then his first mate, Tirrell, would relieve him and drive the boat the rest of the way there. Tirrell especially wanted another crack at Bill Treese, who had insulted him the other day and cast him adrift when they tried to parlay with them.

He looked at his GPS to make sure he didn't change anything, but the boat was on autopilot and was on course. The seas were calm and the night air was balmy. The moon was almost full. He sighed. *It would be great fun to kill them all and relieve them of any treasure they were bringing up, he thought.*

****

About that time, Captain Lester Smith was looking at the moon from the helm of his ship. He and his crew were going to one of the outer islands. One of their scouts had spotted a civilian party boat with several men and women on it, drinking, dancing and having a good time. He wanted to make a quick score, like he had done the other day. They had searched all day on their island for the opening to the tunnel that would lead them to the treasure cave, but had once again come up empty handed. So, they needed to make some money, and they were told that this would be a good opportunity.

He piloted his air-sea rescue boat toward the yacht he hoped would still be there by dawn. Early morning raids were usually the best when everyone was sleeping, especially if they were hungover.

****

Bill was in his cabin, looking at the six daggers which all looked lethal in many ways. There was the obvious sharpness of the blades. They had been honed like razors and could likely be used to shave a man's beard, or a woman's legs. Of course, in addition to that, there were the symbols which promised death to anyone who liberated or held these knives.

Ai Yi Yi!, thought Bill. The symbols were the same. Same death threats, same intimidation. *Maybe bad,* he thought, *maybe just bullshit. Guns worked. Holy water worked. Prayer worked. What didn't work for him was superstition and more B.S.*

There was a knock on his cabin hatch. "Enter!" he yelled out.

Manolo came in carrying a plate full of food, along with two Mexican beers. "Hi *Capitain,*" he said, "you didn't eat anything for dinner earlier, so I brought you some food."

Bill looked down for a second. He almost didn't look up because he was thinking how much he loved this fine young man, who was here to help and take care of him.

"Hi, Manolo. Thank you. I guess I kind of forgot about time for a while."

Manolo set the food down on Bill's bunk. He started to leave.

"Hey, Manolo," Bill said, "stay a minute."

Manolo smiled, always happy to be in Bill's good graces. "Yes *Capitain?*

"So, we have these swords and they say they are going to kill us because we have found them, and they are evil, and mad, and feeling shitty, losing at poker, and have been alone for a long time, and are pissed off at us and the world…," but by then Manolo was cracking up.

"Yes sir, but what are you getting at, *Capitain?*" he smiled and continued to giggle.

"Well, it says we only have to get them back to their owner and all will be forgiven!"

"*Capitain,* how will we do that, since he lived over one hundred and fifty years ago?"

There is another Captain Lester Smith somewhere on Jamaica, but we need to find him."

"*Capitain,* that will be a.., uh, tall order, as you say?"

"Have faith son. Have faith! We've seen worse shit out here in the past two years, right? Don't ask for a miracle if you don't expect one, little *amigo*! Or pray for one!"

"*Si, Capitain.* Can you eat for me please? You need to eat, sir"

Bill sighed and smiled at him. "Ok, son. Ya, I will. Get out of here and get some sleep. Tell Miguel I will come up in a few minutes and relieve him at the helm. He's been working his ass off this whole trip and has been stuck onboard. So, I want to do something for him."

"OK *Capitain!*"

Bill ate the food. It was really good. Manolo had made *bandeja paisa,* which was a really popular Colombian dish, which consisted of beans, rice, chorizo, fried egg, avocado and arepas cheese. There was also grilled beef and fried pork belly, *(chicharrones)*. The food was awesome, and everyone had lapped it up earlier at dinner. Feeling like a stuffed pig, which was not good for war, Bill went up the ladder, carrying his last beer and relieved Miguel.

For a minute, they stayed together at the helm.

Bill spoke first, "Miguel, I know you have only been driving the boat and have not dived with us, but I want you to know you are really important to me. Whatever we bring up, a lot or a little, you will have a full share."

Miguel smiled. He had a family back in Colombia and this meant a lot. "*Gracias,*" he said, smiling.

He wanted to savor the moment and have a little fun. "*Capitain,* is that just the *cerveza* talking, or do you really mean it?" Bill acted like he was going to take a swing at him, but Miguel giggled, ducked under it, and made a hasty retreat below decks to avoid Bill's happy retribution, to eat a little, and then to sleep. Bill smiled, knowing he was very lucky to have such a crew.

The dawn was late. Unexpected clouds came and then there was rain over the Caribbean skies. Bill was at the helm. With Manolo's help, he had put up a canvas covering over the bridge, which helped but did not shelter them completely from the elements.

He was heading for the coast to pick up fuel and supplies as they were running low.

The gold he had gotten from the sunken ship was wonderful, but it didn't buy squat out here! Only hard currency bought them the things they needed.

It was about two hours later that they spotted them. In

fact, no one knew who spotted each other first.

Bill was looking through his binoculars at the boat on the horizon.

At the same time, Captain Lester Smith was looking through his binoculars at the other boat on the horizon, hoping it might be an easy mark as the one they were looking for had apparently gotten away.

Lester saw that it was a boat going fast, but he couldn't tell what kind of boat it was.

"Trinidad!" he shouted, "Turn 90 degrees starboard and let's go after these fat poppin' jays! Raise the Jolly Roger flag so they know we are pirates!"

One of the men grabbed the halyard and raised the black flag with the white skull and crossbones symbol, with a red bandanna on top of the skull, to tell their intended targets they were about to attack.

"Aye sir," was Trinidad's response. He called out to the crew, "On your guns, maties! We attack in a few minutes!"

Bill, looking out at the boat approaching them, realized it was an air-sea rescue boat from World War II, similar to his PT boat, only smaller, and with less weaponry. But it was flying toward them as though it was going to attack. But attack what? Why? They had nothing anyone would want. He could see the tell-tale black flag flying in the breeze as the pirate boat flew at them at high speed!

"Capitain," Manolo spoke up, what do you want me to do?"

Bill sighed. Once again in harm's way. He hit the Battle

Stations alarm and up came Jack, Kimmi, John and Miguel.

"Manolo," Bill said, "get in the starboard gun. Jack, please go to the port gun. Miguel, you are on the Oerlikon cannon in the stern, but there is no protection there, so if there is gunfire, get away from it anyway you can. John and Kimmi, I want you here in the bridge with me, behind the armor. Not sure who these new jokers are, but we need to be ready for them."

They all put on their helmets and life jackets. They took their positions as the air-sea rescue boat charged closer and closer.

Suddenly, the air-sea rescue boat opened fire on the PT boat, with what appeared to be deck cannons! Their aim was bad, likely due to the high speed they were approaching the PT boat.

Bill turned the boat to face them and increasing his speed to flank, he shouted out to Manolo and Jack.

"Commence firing! Commence firing! Fire at will! Fire at will!"

Both Manolo and Jack racked their twin mounted .50 caliber and began firing directly at the approaching boat.

This was new for Captain Lester, and he rather enjoyed it.

He turned to his first mate Trinidad, "My God, *mon*, they are actually firing back at us! Finally, an opponent who will not lay down and die!" He smiled.

"Bring us about!" Lester cried. " Full cannon barrage!"

They swung around to their left as now the PT boat was approaching them.

Lester's men let go a full round of cannon fire from their starboard side intending to disable and finally kill the PT boat.

But Bill would have none of that. Juking and swerving his boat, he avoided the enemy fire. Unfortunately, by doing this, he also screwed up his own gunner's ability to hit their target and their shots went wild.

The PT boat turned and both boats were running parallel 100 yards apart and firing at each other. Because of the clouds, rain and fog, no one was able to get a clear shot. The waves and heavy surf also bounced the vessels around and they both kept missing their targets.

The air-sea boat was getting closer on its parallel run. It was now two hundred feet from the PT boat. Jack, being the port gunner, fired repeatedly at the side of the pirate's boat, but to no avail. Miguel, on the Oerlikon cannon, was also firing at the air-sea rescue boat, but also missing badly.

The Air-sea rescue boat fired volley after volley at the PT boat, but missed their intended target, time after time.

Both Bill Treese at the helm of the PT boat and Captain Lester Smith had the opportunity to turn their boats around and escape, but neither wanted to surrender. Bill yelled out for everyone to hang on. He suddenly put the PT boat in a power turn to the starboard, or right side, moving away from the battle driving straight for several seconds. Once he was about a quarter of a mile away he turned port, to his left, and drove straight at the pirate's boat which had not changed course.

Captain Lester, at first thought the PT boat was running away, but then he saw them turn and head straight back at them on an intercepting course, as though they were going to crash into him. Suddenly, he realized what the PT boat was attempting to do.

He turned to his first mate Trindad and shouted, "My God, *mon!!* They're going to fire a torpedo at us!"

Just then the tell-tale puff of steam escaped the forward, right torpedo tube and the torpedo shot into the water. Because the pirate's boat was going fast, Bill had to figure where they would be when the torpedo hit its mark. It wasn't an exact science, but it was better than simple dead reckoning. In fact, Bill, looking through his torpedo sight, smiled as he could see that he had made a perfect shot and it was going to hit the pirate's boat just at their amidship.

Captain Lester's men yelled out in unison as they saw what was about to happen, but then to everyone's amazement, their captain turned hard to his left, just as the torpedo was going to hit them. It passed harmlessly to the right side of the bow, as Lester's men hung on for dear life. One of them, Lenny, would have been tossed overboard, had it not been for the quick thinking and even quicker hands of his mate, Thomas, who grabbed him just in time and pulled him back onto the deck.

Captain Lester, kept the wheel turned until they were going 180 degrees back in the direction they came. At the same time, Bill turned his PT boat in the opposite direction. They had all had enough for one day.

John and Kimmi both stood up. What about the torpedo? John asked. Bill pointed to an island about a quarter of a mile away. "Watch," he said. Suddenly, there was a tremendous explosion on a rocky outcropping near a beach. Rocks flew into the air and several palm trees blew apart and fell down into the ocean.

Kimmi covered her mouth with her hand as if trying not to scream, "Oh my Lord!" she exclaimed finally. "Anybody live there?" she asked.

Bill shook his head, "No, it's deserted." He looked around

at the others. We need to get to the mainland for supplies and," he hesitated, "another damn torpedo. I'll radio ahead to see if something is available, from my, uh, supplier."

He yelled over to Jack, Manolo and back to Miguel, "Secure Battle Stations. All hands stand down! Manolo, can you make us some lunch, please? Miguel, can you please drive the boat while I make a phone call? I'll give you the course. Thank you everyone, once again. I thought this was just going to be a simple treasure hunt!" he exclaimed, before shaking his head.

Bill looked over at John, who shrugged his shoulders. Ever the scholar, John said, "There is a Greek Proverb that says, 'Where there is a sea there are pirates.'"

Bill nodded, upset with the senseless attack on his crew and his vessel, "Let's get the hell out of here!" he said.

Captain Lester Smith was still trying to get his head around what had just happened. That was the first time they had ever been challenged. Most others just flopped down and handed over their money. *That torpedo was damn close, he thought.* When it hit the island, he was shocked at how much power there was on detonation. Had he not been as skilled a driver of his boat, they would all have been blown to bits! For now, they needed to get to their own port for food and supplies, before they returned to the safety of their island.

Captain Lester looked over at his first mate Trinidad, who was checking out one of the cannons on the foredeck with one of their men. It had evidently misfired during the exchange and they were trying to fix it.

Lester called out to him, "Trinidad, *mon*, come here

please!"

Trinidad looked up and nodded.

He came to the bridge and stood beside Lester. "Ya, Captain?"

"Whatcha' think about them torpedo, *mon?*" asked Lester.

Trinidad shrugged his shoulders. "Don't know Captain. Bad fish! Could blow us up next time, ya. Maybe go find some fluffy, fat American yachts with no guns!" he smiled, "But I'm not afraid of them, mind you, Captain!" he saluted Captain Lester, who he had been friends with since they were boys in Jamaica.

Lester smiled, "Ya, *mon.* Easier pickings out there." He looked out at the horizon thoughtfully. "But it was great fun, *mon!* Finally found a man who would challenge me! Rare this day, ya!"

Trinidad shook his head and smiled, "Fun for you! I would like a little peace. Maybe open that primary school in Jamaica you always wanted to start? You could be the headmaster and I could be the principal! Live out our days quietly and teach the children to be good!"

Lester looked at his friend for a long time, "It takes money, *mon,* to start and run a school. We need a stake, and that's what we're looking for."

Trinidad nodded. He left the bridge and went back to the sailor who was trying to repair the deck cannon.

Bill had taken over the helm from Miguel after he alerted his supplier that he needed another torpedo. He was told to go ahead and dock in the usual place and stay overnight. He would get it by the next morning or afternoon. Bill knew that it would probably be afternoon and they would have to stay ashore one more night.

Miguel came up topside through the hatch leading down through the charthouse to the small galley, "Lunch is ready, sir!" Miguel saluted him sharply.

Bill smiled, "It's okay Miguel, you eat first and no need to salute me!"

Miguel smiled, "It is OK, *Capitain,* I ate while I was helping Manolo make the food. You go ahead," he started to salute again, but pulled his hand back with his other hand, as if it was a great effort to do so. He acted like his hands were fighting each other to salute or not salute. Bill laughed and shook his head. He switched places with Miguel, and ducking, disappeared into the charthouse and descended down the ladder.

Kimmi, John, and Jack were sitting at the small table eating while Manolo stood next to the stove. Bill walked up to the counter. He looked into the large pan. "Ah," he said, "chicken tacos!"

"No, *Capitain, tacos de pollo!*"

"What's that mean?" asked Bill.

"Chicken tacos," was Manolo's quick reply. They all laughed.

Bill picked up four of them. The corn tortillas were not that big, but they were loaded with shredded chicken that had been cooked in chicken stock, with cumin, oregano, garlic, chili powder, crumbled queso fresco, cilantro and a special tomatillo salsa, that Manolo had learned from his grandmother. There was also refried beans, that Bill took a heaping helping of, along with Spanish rice and some sliced lime wedges.

Bill took a bite out of one, with the sauce dripping down

his hand, landing onto the middle of the beans. *That would add more flavor,* he thought. "Oh, man this is good!" he said.

The others all nodded, but were too busy devouring the tacos to say anything. Finally, they all finished and were patting their stomachs contentedly. Kimmi and Manolo both yawned. Even Jack and John looked tired after the events of the morning.

Bill smiled, "Why don't you guys take a nap and sleep for a while. We won't make it to shore for another three hours. If we run into any more bad guys, I'll alert you. Miguel and I can drive the boat. He likes to talk about his escapades with all the girls he has dated, which I have not. He keeps me awake!" he said good-naturedly. They all nodded their heads gratefully and moved to their bunks for some much-needed shut-eye.

****

Angel Rameriez and his party of mercenaries, had arrived near the Blue Hole and were delighted to find that Bill Treese and his crew were nowhere to be seen. He really didn't care. No one could stop them from diving the Hole and looking around. His men were all expert divers and had combat training. They would be using mixed gasses called nitrox, which was, in this case, mixed at 36 percent oxygen in addition to air in their scuba tanks, which allowed them to stay down longer and search deeper. They also had pony air packs which carried an extra amount of emergency air. Finally, they had lined down tanks with regulators at various depths, designed to be used for decompression stops as they came up. Because of the depths and time allowed for the dive, they anticipated decompression stops on their way back up. It took longer, but was much safer for the divers.

Angel was not a diver and would stay with his boat. They had an advanced underwater communication system, full face masks, and could practically talk to each other underwater.

The six divers were geared up and ready to drop into the water. They had made their plans in a "chalk talk" session earlier. They would descend as far as they could and stay down as long as possible. They were hoping to see if Bill Treese and his party had left any clues about the treasure they hoped to find there.

Angel went to the dive master, who was also his first mate, Tirrell, and gave him the signal to dive. On his command, they all jumped forward off the boat and into the sea. For a minute they gathered over the center of the Blue Hole and then, raising the air vent of their buoyancy control life vests over their head and pushing in the plunger that would allow the air to escape, they began to slip below the surface and slide into the sea.

As they descended, they shined their powerful dive lights around the cavern. Other than a ton of fish, they didn't see a lot of what they were looking for, which was gold, a sunken ship or the entrance to a gold tunnel. They were down around 65 feet.

Suddenly, Tirrell spotted the large flat rock, which the sailing vessel had been laying on for two centuries before the storm knocked it off. He immediately swam over to investigate. He touched the surface. It was surprisingly absent of dirt, sand or debris. This rock outcropping would be perfect to hold or hide a ship here.

They had brought ground penetrating sonar, as well. Two of the divers had swam deeper and saw part of the lost ship, which was laying below the ledge against the sloping rock wall of the Blue Hole.

Communicating with each other, they all descended on the back hull of the ship. They surrounded it. There were no masts, spar, or even the front half of the ship. The way it had fallen, it would be easy to access the hold and the officer's quarters, which was usually in the aft, or back section of the boat.

Tirrell signaled to his men. He sent two of them to the top of the shelf with the ground piercing sonar. He and the other three divers swam into the hold of the ship, which was laying on its side because the keel had gotten stuck on the rocks. He was the dive master for a reason; he knew the boat laying on its side, on the rocks, was unstable.

He said to his three divers, "This sonofabitch is really unstable." They all had dived on wrecks in the past and knew the dangers involved. Tirrell led them in. They swam through the hold, with a tow rope behind them attached to a rock on the outside of the vessel, so they could find their way back. First, they found themselves in the hold of the vessel, which was remarkably intact in spite of the fact it was probably over two hundred years old and had recently crashed off the shelf above. They had deducted that.

They flashed their dive lights around, but the hold was empty. Tirrell said, "Let's move back toward the captain's quarters."

On the way back, they passed the first officer's quarters, the ship doctor, and the master's mate. Finally, they reached what appeared to be the captain's quarters. They shined the light around and actually saw the area where something large had been dragged out and probably removed. The deck was scraped and it looked like there had been a chest of some kind, but it was not there now. Tirrell communicated this to the other divers, and of course Angel could hear the communication.

Angel talked over his radio, "Look around. There may be more! Check the other cabins as well!" but he knew only the Captain would have possession of the money and any and all treasure.

"Negative," said Tirrell after a few minutes of search. "There is nothing else down here. Whatever may have been here is long gone." He heard Angel yell, "Fuck!" and nothing else.

Topside, Angel ripped his headset off and threw it across the cabin in anger. "Fucking Bill Treese!" he screamed into his hands. He suddenly got an idea. He picked up the headset, but only held one side to his ear and spoke through the microphone.

"Tirrell, check the doctor's quarters. Be really thorough. Look everywhere, even if you have to tear the bunk apart!"

Tirrell looked around at his men, who were floating near him. "Do it," he said. One went inside and the other two stayed in the hallway because the quarters were incredibly tight, as you would expect on a sailing vessel from the nineteenth century. The diver suddenly held up his hand. He reached for his knife and began to cut away at something under the bunk. He indicated he wanted the other two divers to flood the cabin with light, which they did. He began to pull a long, black metal box out from under the bunk. He brought it out to Tirrell.

Tirrell said into the microphone, "We've got something."

"Bring it up," said Angel.

"Roger that. Let me talk to my two sonar guys on the ledge."

They all swam out of the hold of the ship and met up with the two soldiers who were exploring the ledge.

Tirrell spoke up, "What do you have?" he asked. Both of them were going over and over the base of the rocks.
"There is something here, sir!" said one of the men.

Tirrell checked his dive tables. Even with the oxygen and the extra air, they had been down a really long time. They would have to decompress, which would not make Angel happy, because he wanted to see what they had found right away. Reluctantly, giving into a demanding boss, he called them off the shelf. Dutifully, he called up to Angel, "Sir, we have found a box in the doctor's quarters."

Quick was Angel's reply, "Bring it up to me at once!"

Tirrell rolled his eyes, "Sir, we have to make decompression stops to avoid the bends, sir."

Angel, who had done two lines of coke and shot up an injection of heroin, while the others were diving, had zero rationale about him.

"Bring it up now!" he screamed.

Tirrell knew he had the safety of his men in his hands said, "Negative, sir. We will decompress and be up in one hour, maybe less. The sonar men have found what may be a tunnel down here going into the rock. Should they stay and explore it, sir? It will take some more time?"

"Negative?!" Angel screamed into the microphone, "Get your fucking asses up here now or as soon as you can! We'll come back later!"

Tirrell rolled his eyes. "Aye, aye, sir," he knew it was a mistake. What his sonar men had found could be the tunnel they were looking for, but if he disobeyed Angel, he might get shot as he emerged from the water. That wasn't a chance he was willing to take. He swam over to the two on the ledge. "Can you make out the entrance?"

"Negative, sir," one of them said, "but I know it is right about here," he said pointing to a rather distinct depression in the rocks, which looked almost like a fresh hole that had been dug up and then filled in.

"Do you have paint?" asked Tirrell, meaning underwater paint to mark a spot they needed to locate when they came back.

"Roger that, sir!"

"OK, mark it."

Satisfied, Tirrell made a motion with his thumb to ascend to the surface, but they would make decompression stops along the way.

Angel had passed out, sleeping in the cozy arms of Morpheus, but after an hour had awakened suddenly. Just then Tirrell and his men had made it to the boat and were climbing aboard. Angel came out onto the deck, and, as if to make up for his earlier bad behavior, helped the men take off their scuba gear and place it onto the deck.

He went up to Tirrell. "Do you have the box you recovered?" he asked.

Tirrell nodded his head, still pissed off. "Yeah," he brought the doctor's box out of his dive bag.

Angel smiled. He motioned for Tirrell to go below with him. They descended the ladder and went into his quarters. They placed the box on Angel's desk. Using a pocket knife, Angel expertly opened the box. They looked at it eagerly. There were several large vials of some substances, some clear and some smokey. They obviously were drugs, but they didn't know what kind they were. Angel smiled. There was money in liquid gold too!

Angel turned to Tirrell, "Tell your men good job. Let's make for port and get these meds checked out. It has to be morphine and a lot of it. This could be a million bucks worth!" he said excitedly.

Tirrell shrugged his shoulders and said, "OK." *What about the underwater tunnel?* he thought. *Dumb shit! That's where the treasure is at, and the real money!"*

Bill and the crew had reached the mainland by that afternoon. They tied up and made plans to go into town for some food and drinks. There was a café in town they had frequented before. They were all going to go, but Miguel had sent a message to his family and wanted to wait at the boat to hear from them. Bill thought this was probably prudent, to have a sentry present on the PT boat. He promised to bring him back something good from the restaurant and some local beer, which was awesome.

They all showed up at the café and sat in a large patio with a big fan beating overhead.

Bill decided to order for everyone because he knew the place well and was friends with the owner. This cut down on the chances of bugs, poison, hair or blood being in the food, he told them. Everyone responded by looking slightly sick until Bill laughed and told them it was just a joke.

Bill ordered several *Antarctica Original* beers, which packed a punch, but was really smooth on a warm night, like tonight. He ordered two orders of *moqueca*, which was piping hot fish stew served in a clay pot; *pao de queijo*, which was cheese and bread rolls, crispy on the outside and soft on the inside; *feijoada*, a hearty stew of sausage, black beans, with rice, farofa and kale. The hard drinks were *cachaca*, Brazil's national cocktail, distilled from fermented sugarcane juice, mixed with local juices, and rum for an added kick.

They all ate and drank well into the night. They were a little drunk, but no one lost control, because they knew things could or would get rough at a moment's notice. Bill himself packed up a really nice dinner for Miguel and took him back some cocktails.

They returned to the boat, talked for a while, then everyone went to bed. Bill stayed up and would drink coffee for a while and stand watch until dawn. He was used to it. The drinks were good, but he had a job to do and could not afford to get sloppy. Manolo and Miguel would relieve him then, so that they would get some good rest tonight.

Bill had heard from his military supplier that the replacement torpedo would be delivered tomorrow, around midnight, which meant that they would stay another night in port. The longer they remained there, the more dangerous it was. Locals would sniff them out and possibly try to attack the boat. If the truth be known, when the PT boat was out of the water, so to speak, she had less than one-half her fire power, without the torpedoes or the depth charges.

So, they needed to get back to sea as soon as possible. They also needed to get back to the area around the Blue Hole and look for the island where they saw the end of the treasure tunnel. Bill wanted to look for the mysterious Captain Lester Smith, who may or may not still exist. All the bullshit aside, Bill would still like to get that curse off of their heads—even though it was probably just a hoax. He smiled. He was actually thinking about the curse. He rolled his eyes. *Might as well commit me,* he thought. *OK. Fuck it. Maybe there was some sort of curse. Best to just tend to business and the curse be damned. Meet it head on, like he had always handled all of his problems! Good time to pray. Then move on!*

Bill sat back in the deck captain's chair and took a long slug of coffee. They were docked and not moving. Looking out at the Caribbean Sea, it wasn't the same as navigating up the Amazon. Nor was it the same as truly moving into combat. He hated that. He felt like a sitting duck while they were tied up here. But this was better than the alternative. He did not desire a nice porch with a nice big rocking chair he could retire on. Probably not going to happen.

He thought about the pirates they had encountered earlier that day. *Who the hell were they? Why were they coming for the PT boat? Bill and his crew had no money or valuables. The PT boat was clearly a more dangerous target, way more so than the air-sea rescue boat which was assigned to rescue downed American pilots during WWII. There were arms aboard their vessel but the PT boat was a warship with machine guns, cannons, torpedoes and depth charges. There was no comparison.*

The air-sea rescue boat had been retrofitted with cannons, but Bill did not know what kind. Due to the weather, the rough seas, the bad shooting and the fact that they had missed their target with the torpedo, there had been no casualties.

But, he asked himself, *what about next time?*

Bill sat back in his chair. It was going to be a long night.

****

Angel's first mate, Tirrell, had spoken to Angel about what

they were going to do, going forward. They couldn't risk another dive, or could they? Angel had come down from his previous high and was considering everything that was being proposed to him.

There was an obvious chamber of air behind where the wreck had rested before it was thrown off the reef, but no one knew how to make access to it and find the tunnel. They had marked the spot with paint and Tirrell wanted to return and explore there. Angel thought about that, but had a feeling the PT boat would return soon. He had another plan in mind.

Angel said, "We will go to our island and sell the drugs. Then we will retreat to observe where and when they will reenter the water. Then we will make our move. We will attack and kill them underwater! Then we will explore your cave of treasure and keep it all for ourselves!"

Tirrell nodded his head. They thought this would be an excellent plan.

****

Bill Treese had been relieved by Manolo around 0600, went below and immediately fell asleep in his bunk. He slept hard and fast, but dreamed much. His subconscious felt the negative energy from the six swords that lay below him, under his bunk. They were cursed, and maybe he was too. In his dream he was being pursued by a large dark- skinned man, with a giant beard, in pirate garb. He was trying to catch Bill and kept screaming, *Give me my swords back!,* over and over again. But Bill had left them on the boat and this man couldn't hear him, even though Bill was yelling that he didn't have them, and it went on and on. Bill, semiconscious, yelled, "I don't have them!" which suddenly woke him up and, if it had not been for the steel bulkhead door of Bill's cabin, would have frightened his crew.

So, he sat up, rubbing his eyes. He looked at his watch. 12:00 noon straight up. Time to get up, get coffee and take over the helm. He got out of bed, used the head, dressed and went out to the galley. Happily, there was fresh coffee, which he downed two cups in less than two minutes. He saw bacon, fried eggs and English muffins sitting on the counter. He made a sloppy sandwich, with ketchup and grease dripping off the side. He ate it quickly, slammed a can of orange juice and then went topside.

Once he climbed up the ladder, Bill looked around. He squinted his eyes against the bright sun. He could see Manolo working on the Oerlikon cannon, oiling it and checking the magazine. Jack, Kimmi and John were on the deck next to the day cabin with a large map spread out over the roof of the day cabin and were pouring over it. Miguel, was laying on the foredeck, shirt off and pants rolled up, sleeping like a cat in the sun.

Bill walked over to John, Jack and Kimmi, "Hi guys, any luck?"

They all looked up. "Hope you slept OK," said John. "You looked tired as hell last night!"

"Yeah, I guess I did at that," he smiled. "What are you guys doing, anyway?"

Jack spoke up, "We're trying to figure out which island might be the connection for the cave. We are pretty sure it is this one," he said pointing to one about a mile and a half from the Blue Hole. "It looks like there may be some kind of waterway inlet that would shelter people and maybe a boat. But, if so, we need to make an approach as soon as possible because the element of surprise has eluded us so far!"

Bill smiled, "You are right, Jack. As soon as we get our torpedo, we're out of here!

He turned to Kimmi, "Can you, John and Manolo go into town and buy this from the Green Market?" He handed her a big grocery list of food items and three $100.00 bills. The store is about a block past the café we were at last night. It will probably be around 250 bucks. Tell them to keep the change. Tell them it's from Big Bill. They know me!" He smiled. "They will deliver it in a couple of hours, so you don't have to lug it back to the boat." Kimmi nodded and she, her dad and Manolo walked down the gangplank onto the sand and left for the village.

Later that evening, after eating chili, cheese and corn chips prepared by Manolo, they all waited on deck for the torpedo to arrive. It was 10:00 p.m. and Manolo was the first to hear the low rumblings of the small motor pushing the barge along. *"Capitian,"* he said, "They are here!"

Bill, who was sitting on the captain's deck chair, said, "OK, lively boys. They are going to wench this fish up to us, but we have to load it into the torpedo tube. It is heavy and dangerous. Please don't drop the F'in' thing! It'll make a big noise and ruin our day!"

The others laughed a little, but not much. They wanted to get this weapon aboard and get the hell out of here. Bill had told them earlier he wasn't going to spend another night in this port. Once they loaded the fish, they were going to leave, with some sleeping below and others standing watch in the gun turrets all night.

The barge pulled alongside the PT boat and threw a line up to Manolo, who was on the bow, and another to Miguel, who was standing on the stern. They both tied the barge off as the boat operator cut the engines. It was eerily quiet in the dark, with the small wake from the barge slapping against the hull of the PT boat.

Manolo and Miguel jumped over onto the barge and helped the two mates set up the wench needed to move the torpedo, which weighed over 1,000 pounds, into position.

It took about 30 minutes, with both Jack and John lending a hand, with Bill directing them. It was still hot, even though it was late at night, and everyone was sweating profusely. Bill said, "Ram that charge easy, please. Go soft and please make it easy. We'll tie it off and make it secure ourselves."

Once it was secure, Bill paid the barge operator in cash, and the barge pushed off, disappearing back into the dark night.

John came up to Bill, "Just out of curiosity, what does one of those bastard's cost?" he asked.

Bill looked at him, "In these parts, $25,000 buys one torpedo. That's considered a bargain. Any other questions?"

John shook his head. "I'm sorry Bill. Let's hope we get something to pay for this excursion." Bill shook his head and looked disgusted.

Bill told them to make a final check of the torpedo and made preparations to get underway. Firing up the engines, he told Jack and John get on the two twin machine guns and told Manolo, Kimmi, and Miguel, to go below and get some sleep. He told them to come up in about six hours and take a turn on the guns. That way, Miguel could take over at the helm, Kimmi could man a machine gun and Manolo would make breakfast unless she wanted to trade places with him.

Kimmi smiled at Bill, "I think Manolo is a better cook than I am," she said, "But in a pinch I could pull it off!"

Bill laughed, "OK, it's almost midnight, so you guys get some sleep! We should be near the Hole by the time you guys wake up. We'll see you in a few hours."

They nodded and went below.

Miguel had separate sleeping quarters, leaving Kimmi and Manolo alone in the forecastle, or the bow of the boat. Normally, they would leave the hatch open, but Kimmi closed it and turned the wheel to lock it. She turned to Manolo. She walked up to him and looked into his eyes. "I've wanted this chance since we landed here," she said.

Manolo smiled and kissed her tenderly on the lips. He took her in his arms and they kissed passionately.

Kimmi looked into his eyes, "Let's be good to each other, tonight," she whispered.

Manolo smiled and they moved toward his bunk. They undressed quickly and got under the covers, both naked. Manolo kissed her and felt the thrill as she French kissed him for the first time. He touched her breasts with passion. She reached down and curled her hand around his manhood and began to guide him into her.

"Oh, Kimmi," he said as they began to make love.

Six hours later, Kimmi bounded up the ladder, happily to the deck. She smiled at everyone, "Good morning! Reporting as ordered!"

Bill smiled, pointing at her dad and Uncle Jack, who were

both sound asleep, each laying across their twin machine guns.

Kimmi laughed.

"I didn't have the heart to wake them up," Bill said. "Plus, there was nothing happening. We are almost at the Blue Hole and, all of you guys needed sleep. I'll go below as soon as Miguel comes up and sleep for a couple of hours. Then we should be approaching our target. It'll be OK, I don't need much sleep."

"OK," said Kimmi, "what is the plan when we get there?"

I want to make one more dive and explore the treasure chamber. Then, I might blow the entrance to the tunnel," he paused, "Maybe. We'll see."

Just then Miguel came up on deck. "Ready to relieve you, *Capitan!* Go get some sleep. Manolo will have breakfast when you get up!"

"Thanks Miguel," said Bill. He was really tired. He descended down the ladder and saw Manolo bustling around the galley, making breakfast. Without even saying hi, Bill went into his cabin and fell into his bunk. He was asleep immediately and did not wake up for over two hours.

****

Captain Lester Smith was in his cabin on his air-sea Rescue boat, tied up to the dock on his island. He had his great grandpa's diary out again. His first mate, Trinidad, was with the crew, continuing to look for the opening in the rocks that would lead to the secret treasure cave, that had eluded them for over 150 years. He turned to the entry that his great grandpa, also known as Captain Lester Smith, Esq., had written about his only real naval defeat in all the years he was a pirate:

"Diary entry, July 22, 1869, going forward:

On the frigate vessel, JAMAICAS REVENGE, with 28, 24-pounder cannons, on each side, plus four long nine, 9-pounders, fore and aft. My crew was only 40 men, plus the officers. We were a skeleton crew, because some of our mates had been injured and killed. I feel sad when I have to perform the burials at sea and bring the flag of Jamaica back to the families. It is my honor. It is my duty. They died in our service, but I bear a weight that I will never be shed of. If I had done this or that differently, they might still be alive. No one blames me. I blame myself, and this, I must bear as Captain. All brave men, leaving brave families behind.

This morning the sun was up early, but was filtering through thick storm clouds. I knew it was going to be a heavy storm we were heading into. Yesterday, we had been chased by two Union war ships. We had a lusty exchange of cannon fire, but no casualties on either side, although we had fired a cannon ball that went through one of their mainsails, but did not hit the deck. The seas were rough. The wind had come up from the south quarter and made sailing our ship very hard. They pursued us for over an hour. Finally, we got away far enough. I was mad. I did not want to leave this unfinished. So I turned the ship around and sailed at them firing the fore cannons. It must have taken them by surprise because they had not loaded properly and could not return fire while we sailed between them firing a full volley broadside. The damn seas continued to roll and we missed those bastards at point-blank range. The fog was setting and we sailed into it before they could return fire or come back at us.

We slept with the standard watch, expecting them to enter our fog cover, but they didn't. At six bells, we started back out to hunt them. They were between us and Jamaica.

Now we were sailing out of the fog bank and the darkness of the night. After two hours, we spotted them on the horizon. We set full sail, heading into battle. After a few minutes, they spotted us and turned to face us.

The rain started coming down and made it harder to see them. Also, the clouds were descending, even though the fog was behind us, we could see another fogbank behind them. The wind was at our back and we closed the distance quickly. We tried to pass between them, but they fell into single file. So much the better, my first mate said to me. I yelled for the men to stand to their arms and prepare to fire a volley at the first vessel. I sent the rest of the men to the other side of the ship because I knew their tactics and they would split up at the last second and try to hit us from both sides at once. I also had men on the fore and aft cannons ready to fire.

As I expected, the trailing vessel crossed our bow, and my men on both sides of the bow fired a volley which hit them broadside. They fired back at us, but most *missed. Our fore cabin was hit, but was not destroyed. The first ship passed us on our starboard side firing a full volley, and we returned fire with our 24 pounders to a full pattern. Both of us hit our mark, with them getting the worst of it. Their ship was on fire and began to list toward us, to their starboard, as me men fired more which hit their decks and forced them to begin sinking, making their cannons useless. We were only a few meters away and some of their men leaped aboard my vessel with pistols, rifles and swords. My men rose up to fight them hand to hand. There were casualties on both sides and because of the seas, the deck began to pitch and roll. I leapt out of the bridge, leaving my quarter master, who had taken over the helm, while the helmsman and seamen began to repel the boarders onto our vessel. I leapt on top of several of the enemy and killed them all with my cutlass.*

Suddenly, I realized the trailing ship which had crossed our bow and had taken several hits from our 9-pounders was pulling up next to our port side. Both ships fired a full volley at point-blank range, succeeded in critical damage to both vessels. Both Union vessels sank almost immediately. My main mast had been blown off and fire was everywhere. I saw no survivors on either vessel, but many of my men, who had killed the Union boarders, were screaming to abandon ship. We had one life boat left, the others had been destroyed in the battle, but it would not hold all of us. I ran over and cut the line to the boat, but my ship was listing so badly, the life boat was already touching the water. Fire was everywhere, only dampened somewhat by the rain.

I yelled for them to jump in the water and then retrieve the life boat. We all jumped in the ocean. Me men swam and jumped on board the life boat. As I swam, I encountered some of the rigging, which had one of the foresails still attached to one of the cross pieces. I began to push it ahead of me moving toward the life boat and me men. Several saw me and jumped into the water and helped me get it to the life boat. We dragged it to the boat, knowing we might need it to navigate. There was enough room in the boat. Only 12 of us had survived out of 45 total crewmen and I was sad.

Suddenly, we heard a loud crack and crash as the fore and rear masts crashed into the sea! As we looked out, our beautiful frigate ship, JAMAICAS REVENGE, slipped below the waves and was lost to us forever. None of me men looked at me as tears fell from my eyes. I had let them all down and was responsible for this naval disaster. Me men knew me well. I loved my ship as I loved all of them. Every disaster was a scar on my heart. I would take every man's name in my service, alive or dead, to me grave.

I did not have the luxury of dwelling on my loss. I had to save me men. They were looking at me to do something. I stood on the bow and held my eyepiece up. There was nothing but ocean, fog and rain. We were adrift with only four oars left in the oarlocks because the other four had either broken up or fallen off. I felt we were in some type of current or tide, but several tymes the ocean broke over us, drenching me and me men. After about two hours, it was late afternoon and the skies began to clear. The rain stopped and the sun came out. On the horizon, my first mate, yelled he saw land dead ahead of us. Though there were still some clouds, the fog was gone and the visibility was returning. We could see a tall single peak, which looked like a small volcano. I could see breakers ahead of us, and I knew we would be thrashed if we tried to make the beach.

I told me men to row parallel to the beach beyond the breakwater. We rowed around, still towing the broken rigging behind us. Finally, we saw an inlet with calm water, which led back to what looked like the base of the mountain. We steered up the channel of water and into a cave. The cavern was dark, so we moved back out and left the boat for the beach.

Our first matter was survival. As we explored around, we found streams of water coming off the mountain and pooling into a fresh water pool next to the beach, which then emptied into the bay. We all drank gratefully. We found groves of mangoes, bananas, and coconut trees. All of the men, even those who were wounded in battle, helped to gather food. We had nothing to hold the water in, so we cracked open some coconuts, drank the milk, scooped out the meat, and used them to bring water. The night was warm, but we built a fire, as the cook had brought flint and steel. We thought we would try to fish in the morning and some fashioned spears out of our knives and swords because we had no hooks or line to fish with.

We were there two weeks. We had found a passage back into the very interior of the island, under the mountain. It went way back and we knew we were now under the ocean. Our compass told us we were headed back towards where our ship had sunk. We found a large chamber and then a short tunnel beyond which led to a hole in the floor, filled with water.

By then, we had rigged the sail on the life boat. We loaded up the boat with water, fruit and fish. We had evaporated sea water to get the salt, which we rubbed into the cooked fish to preserve it. We had enough supplies for two weeks at sea. By using the stars to navigate, we reached Jamaica in eight days, thanks to a good wind and good seas.

I had to face a military tribunal, fully expecting to be court-marshaled, as I should have been, but they pinned a medal on me and told me and me men, we were heroes for defeating two Union frigates, which were much larger and had more fire power than us. Also, for getting the sailors back to our island safely. No one died on the way back to Jamaica, even the ones with battle wounds.

We were outfitted with another vessel, named JAMAICAS REVENGE II. We eventually made it back to the island, which we used as a base, to launch raids on the enemy. That is where we knew we could hide a great amount of the treasure, along with sharing much *of it with our government. They did not demand all of it. They knew we were the ones risking our lives, so they were kindly. They assisted us in getting a new vessel and so the raids would continue.*

For many years, we wreaked havoc on the enemy. By nature, we were peaceful men, but they had brought it upon themselves to go into harm's way to try to seek their revenge. We made them realize their revenge and their arrogance that we were just dumb negros, and they were brilliant white men, was very expensive to them in both money and lives. Bastards all! May they burn in Hell!

Captain Lester Smith, the great grandson of the legendary Captain Lester Smith, Esq., touched the words with his fingers. Holding his hand over the special pages, he closed his eyes and breathed in deeply. He then shut the diary and smiled.

His great grandpa was a hero to the people. He wanted them to know about him and his great deeds It was important to the history of their island. *He had to find that passage to the treasure!* he thought, *That was the secret to everything that would lead to greatness and the salvation that was to come to him and his men!*

CHAPTER SIX

THE UNDERWATER DEMOLITION TEAM

MIGUEL SAW THE BLUE HOLE AREA identified by the islands that surrounded it. As instructed earlier by Bill, he stopped the boat and signaled to the others that they needed to eat because they were almost there. They all went down to the galley except Miguel. He couldn't leave his post until Bill came back up on deck and took over.

While they were eating, Manolo knocked on Bill's hatch, which was actually partly open. Bill had been so tired he hadn't even bothered to close the door behind him when he fell asleep. *"Capitain,"* he said softly. "Breakfast, sir."

Bill had been dreaming again about the giant Jamaican pirate, with long dreadlocks, holding a cutlass sword, and Bill was about to be attacked by him! Bill suddenly jumped out of his bunk and, with a yell, landed like a cat on his feet, looking around wildly.

Manolo, startled, backed up and fell backwards, tripping

on the raised edge of the waterproof hatch. He yelled out, startling everyone in the galley. They all jumped up and came over to Manolo. They saw Bill looking around, still dreaming.

Suddenly, Bill woke up and looked out at all the startled faces. Blinking, he looked around and gathered himself. "Sorry guys!" he said. I guess too little sleep, combined with too much stress, has gotten to me." He looked out at Manolo, who had been helped to his feet by the others. "I'm sorry, little buddy," he said regretfully.

It was a little awkward, so everyone moved back to their breakfast. Bill walked over to Manolo and patted him on the back, "Sorry again, Manolo. Do I still rate breakfast around here?" he smiled shamefacedly.

Manolo smiled, "*Si, Capitain.* It is OK! I knew you would go back to the bridge, so I made breakfast burritos and a thermos of coffee you can take up with you. If you want, I'll bring it up."

"Thanks Manolo." He hurried up the ladder. He had a very bad feeling about the day ahead, and it wasn't because of the dream he had just had. He thought about the six daggers below in his cabin, lying in the old sea chest, predicting his death.

Bill took over the helm and told Miguel to go below and eat. He said to eat as much as he could because he was not sure when they would eat again. Last night, he told Jack that he would be diving the Blue Hole with him and to eat enough, but not so much that it would impede their dive.

Manolo brought up four breakfast burritos, made with eggs, bacon, cheese and Spanish rice, plus the thermos of black coffee. Bill smiled, took one burrito, poured one cup of coffee and handed the rest back to a very surprised Manolo.

"Bring everyone up on deck, as soon as they are done eating," said Bill.

Manolo could read his skipper's thoughts after all of these years, and he meant immediately. *There would be no wasted time on this dive*, he thought. He hurried below. Within a minute everyone had appeared on deck.

Bill had his back to the wheel and was facing his crew, who had gathered around him. He set his jaw and was going to deliver the news that would not make them happy.

"Jack and I are going to make a final dive on the treasure cave." John started to protest, and Bill cut him off with one sharp look. This was not lost on the others, as everyone knew that Captain Bill was 100 percent in charge of this mission. There would be no arguments, no pleading, no reasoning or second guessing him. Bill's word would be the final say on the matter at hand.

"We might then have to blow up the entrance to keep anyone else out, who may have been here while we were gone. We know about that guy, Angel, who was on the party boat and who threatened to kill us. He has probably dived down the Hole at least once in the past two days. Maybe more. If so, I pray he never made it into what we found. There is also that air-sea boat that attacked us. I don't know who those jokers were, but they are probably around here as well. For a Blue Hole, which was only known for its colorful fish, it has suddenly become a damn dangerous place!"

Bill looked around. Everyone appeared to be stunned. They had all hoped to see the treasure again and to maybe take some of it out for themselves. Bill decided to soften the blow a little. "First, I said, we may blow the entrance, but maybe not. If Jack and I go down and everything is as we left it, then we might be OK. It was hell of lucky for us to find it, when who knows how many divers have been down there in the past 150 years? Not to mention the access from dry land. Why hasn't anyone found that way back in? Does anyone live on that island? If they did, they would be in for one heck of a surprise, right?!"

Bill continued, "John thinks he knows which island Jack and I had climbed up to when we were in the treasure chamber. Right, John?"

John, still a little stunned that they might seal up the entrance with explosives, and not knowing if it would destroy or flood the cavern or not, nodded.

Bill smiled, "You can speak up, John." Bill read his thoughts. "Don't worry, John. I didn't fall off the Underwater Demolition Technology Squad yesterday. I know how much dynamite I would need to cause a 'gentle' explosion." He smiled and everyone laughed. They all relaxed a little.

Bill continued, "We will get the treasure, but who knows who may try to claim it? But we need to get what we need to get and then get the hell out of here, before the bad guys come, savvy?"

The others nodded. Bill smiled, "It will be OK. Here is the plan. Miguel drives us to the site while Jack and I gear up for our dive. Single air tanks only. No dual tanks or nitrogen. We won't be diving that long. Kimmi and John are on the twin machine guns and Manolo is on the Oerlikon Cannon. You can communicate with us through the dive channel communication system. If you see anything, signal us. If any boats appear to be hostile toward you, then prepare to repel boarders. Don't be afraid to shoot! No one around here is friendly. If they were, they wouldn't be here anyway. Right now, it is kill, or be killed! If you have to run, then run! Jack and I can always drift, go into the cave, and maybe force our way onto the island. So which island, John?" he asked.

John didn't hesitate. He pointed to an island that had a thick volcanic rise above sea level. It was about five miles away from them and one and a half miles away from the Blue Hole. "That one," he said, "is the most logical choice and the closest one to us!"

"Thank you," was Bill's reply. "Let's get moving!" They all scrambled into action.

****

Angel Rameriez and his first mate Tirrell made their way back to their yacht. They had learned that the drugs they found on the pirate ship in the doctor's quarters were pure morphine, worth well over two million dollars. They had made a deal to sell it for 1.2 million in cash to some local drug kingpins, which was now in the briefcase Tirrell was carrying. The negotiations had been tough. The drug lord of the island had his own resources. They had met face to face.

Angel and Tirrell had been escorted to a garage where the drug lord, named Joe Mata, had parked his military jeep next to an interior wall. Angel climbed out of his own jeep and stood waiting for the bad guys to emerge. Tirrell was in the back seat, holding an AK-47 fully automatic machine gun.

Finally, Mata and his lead gunner stepped out of their jeep

holding a black briefcase. Two more of his soldiers jumped out of the jeep, holding their own AK-47s and fanned out to either side of the jeep. Mata smiled at Angel. "Do you have the goods?" he asked.

Angel nodded. He reached inside his jeep and pulled out his own briefcase, which was thick and bulky, given the weight of the medication inside.

Mata walked over to Angel's jeep. Angel held up the briefcase, laid it across the hood of the jeep and opened it up. It showed several vials from the pirate ship.

Mata looked at the vials of what he had been told was pure morphine. He glanced up at Angel. "Has it been tested?"

Angel nodded his head. "Yes. Pure morphine that you can cut over and over and still maintain its potency!"

Mata smiled. "May I," he asked pulling out a tester kit.

"Of course," smile Angel, "100 percent pure morphine, without FDA rules from the 1800s!"

Mata took a sample of the liquid and placed it in the tester. He shook it up and it indicated it was pure. He took two more random sample from the other vials and tested them as well. The results were the same. He looked at Angel and smiled. "Sold!"

Everybody relaxed and stood down as the morphine was real. Mata had no reason to rip-off Angel as they had done deals in the past, and they wished to continue doing business together in the future. They could refine the morphine into heroin, cut it, mix it and almost double their money. Plus, it was an easy delivery from a trusted source, without any police encumbrances. It couldn't be more perfect and Mata was once again happy to do an easy drug deal, which would net him well over a million dollars in cash.

****

When Angel and Tirrell reached their boat, they walked up the gangplank and immediately went belowdecks. Angel brought out six hundred thousand and told Tirrell to give one hundred thousand to each one of the men, then return.

In a few minutes, Tirrell returned, "The men are grateful, sir, they say thank you and are in a very happy mood." Angel smiled, "Here is two hundred thousand for you, don't spend it all in one place!"

"Thank you, Captain."

Angel brought out a bottle of Blanton's Single Barrel Bourbon Whisky, worth about $500, and poured them each a generous glass. They toasted their success. After about 15 minutes, Tirrell wanted to bring up the possible treasure cave, but he chose his words carefully.

"Captain, we are pretty sure we found the entrance to the cave. We were all hoping to go back and take another crack at it. The men have heard stories that the treasure there could be worth millions, maybe hundreds of millions, and may date back to the American Civil War!"

Angel sat back in his chair, "So where did it come from?" he asked.

"No one knows. Maybe pirates? Maybe the Civil War Americans or the South American army? Maybe the Jamaicans? But, we would like to go back. We are sure we can find it and maybe discover the treasure."

"Well," said Angel, "you have a point, and we have

discussed this once before. Why else would Bill Treese be there? He's a treasure hunter, not a tourist." They both stood up. Angel said, "Please give the rest of this bottle to the men and tell them to enjoy it and get some rest. I'll meet you on the bridge and we will sail back to the Blue Hole tonight. *Adelante!*"

****

Miguel steered the PT boat expertly near the edge of the Hole. Bill told him how far away he had to be to stay clear of the blast. Bill, turned to Miguel. "You have the command of the bridge, Miguel," he said. "I'll be back." Bill descended the ladder. He called to Jack, who was in the forecastle getting ready.

"Hey, Jack, can you come to my cabin, please?"

Jack came immediately to Bill's cabin. Bill gestured to the door, and Jack closed the hatch. "I wanted to give you a chance to back out if you wanted to," Bill said. "I know we both know how dangerous this could be. We've been gone for two days and things may have changed down there. Plus, we don't really know who we might be fighting."

Jack nodded and smiled, "Get the F out of here, pal, I'm in for the duration! I'm in all the way! There's no one onboard who is a better diver than me, except you! And you can't dive without a buddy diver, so that's out. By the way, do you have any weapons we can take down there with us? Just in case," he added.

"Yes." Bill produced two shark bang sticks, also known as powerheads, which would fire when in direct contact with the target. The shafts themselves were about five feet long and made of light gage steel. At the end was the powerhead made of heavy-duty stainless steel, which held the charge. There was a safety mechanism in place, so that the weapon would not discharge by accident. Bullets fired in the air could travel over one mile, but because water was about 800 times denser, the projectile would only travel a few feet. When the powerhead made direct contact with its intended target, it would force the round back onto a fixed firing pin, which penetrated the primer and caused it to detonate. There was a variety of ammunition cartridges which could be used, from small to very large, depending on the prey. The ammo primer had to be made waterproof, by a variety of things such as rubber, wax or nail polish.

"Nice," whispered Jack. "What kind of ammo?"

"They hold 12-gauge shotgun shells. It'll be enough fire power if we have to use them. The other end is a spear, but it is telescoped into the shaft and you have to use a spring to get it out." Bill demonstrated for Jack. He touched a button and the 5 inch long, deadly looking spear came out of the steel tube. He also showed Jack the cotter pin near the other end, next to the projectile, that had to be pulled out before it would fire.

"Remember, Jack, you have to press hard into your target to detonate it. Getting that close to your target is dangerous in and of itself."

Jack shrugged. "So, we're going to dive, enter the chamber, and then what?"

"We are going after some of the gold bars, to help finance this trip, then return to the boat. If we see anything we don't like, I'm going to wire the opening and set the charge. If I give you the signal that I have lit the charge, you only have five minutes to get out of the water before it detonates. Understand?"

"How big will the detonation be?" asked Jack.

"Bigger than a firecracker and less than C4. But I'm not really worried about the size of the blast, it's the aftermath that you can't control. Walls can crack, tunnels can flood, rocks can shoot upward and there can also be an avalanche. It could even work against us and open the tunnel further, making access easier for the bad guys!"

"What about after the dive?" asked Jack.

"Then we are going to the island and find the real, dry opening to the cave you and I saw from the other side of the rocks."

"OK. When are we going?"

"Now. Let's go suit up. The sooner the better."

They headed up the ladder, with Bill carrying the two bang sticks.

The sun was up and the water was mostly flat. It was 0930 hours, exactly when Bill wanted to start the dive. They had on communication gear, their underwater lights and their bang sticks. Bill had his waterproof bag with the explosives, the detonating cord and the detonator, which he only had to pull on the handle and a spark would move down the wire to the ordinance. Jack was nervous, in spite of himself. He should be back home with his wife and kids, seeing his patients, not out here playing John Wayne and diving with explosives. Bill also had a sense of doom, but tried to hide it. He kept thinking about those damn swords and the curse. He needed to focus.

They were going to enter the water at the stern of the boat, near the smoke generator. That part of the boat was the closest to the water and made for an easier, safer entry. Manolo was on the Oerlikon cannon in the stern, Miguel at the helm, holding the boat steady. John and Kimmi were each in one of the twin machine guns. They were all looking at Bill and Jack. Bill took a deep breath of fresh air. He placed his hands on his buoyancy control vest, his weight belt, with its emergency release from the right side. He placed his regulator in his mouth and took a couple of puffs of air. He looked over at Jack, who was doing the same check-in with his gear. Jack gave Bill the "OK" sign, which meant he was ready to dive. Bill nodded.

Bill entered the water first by holding his hand to his mask and jumping in. Jack followed, once Bill swam a few feet away from where he landed.

They steadied themselves in the water. Bill gave the thumbs down signal, indicating they could descend below the surface. The others on board the boat, turned back to their stations and scanned the horizon for any hostile enemies. Both Kimmi and John racked their .50 caliber machine guns, loading the bullets into the barrels, ready to fire. They checked their jam-free belt bullet loader, which held 1000 rounds of ammo, and was designed to always ensure smooth, continuous firing at over 1,600 rounds per minute. Manolo did the same thing on the Oerlikon cannon in the stern. Miguel steadied the boat, but made sure everything was "hot' in case they had to move out quickly.

****

Angel Rameriez had sailed his fast yacht to within five miles of the Hole, but on the opposite side that the PT boat was on. He stopped far enough away so they would not be spotted. By using his powerful telescope on the bridge, he could see the PT boat clearly. As he watched, two men in scuba gear jumped into the water. He signaled for his own two divers to get into the water immediately. They had underwater electric dive scooters, that would propel them along 30 feet below the surface. Because they were Colombia's version of U.S. Navy SEALs, they were experts in diving, explosives and killing.

They were targeting the two divers from the PT boat. Once they had killed them, they intended to continue exploring the possible entrance to the cave, and then Angel and the rest of his mercenaries would storm the PT boat and blow it out of the water. Angel knew Bill was one of the divers because he wouldn't leave this dive to chance. And once he was neutralized, the PT boat would be at one-quarter of its strength without Bill on board. He smiled, *easy pickings*, he thought.

Once the two divers from Angel's yacht, on their scooters, reached the edge of the Blue Hole, they cut the power and slowly descended. The visibility was good and they did not use their dive lights because it would give them away.

****

Bill and Jack descended as fast as they could, ignoring the sea life around them. They had reached the area where they had found the opening to the cave. As Jack moved forward, Bill suddenly grabbed his arm and held on. Jack turned around and looked at Bill as if to say, *What the hell?*

Bill's eyes were huge and he pointed back to the rock wall.

Suddenly Jack saw it, a large white cross "X" had been painted over the spot which was their entrance to the cave!

"I have to blow it now!" Bill said over his communication channel, but around his regulator mouthpiece. Jack nodded. He did not have any experience with the ordinance Bill had brought, so he just kept watch for him, flashing his powerful dive light around. As usual, there were a million fish, a few sharks, and a bunch of jelly fish, but fortunately, no bad guys.

Bill went to work setting the charges and hooking the long wire to the underwater blasting cap. It took a while, but by then, he had a complete depth charge pattern. He looked up at Jack and held up five fingers, meaning they had five minutes to get out. Jack nodded. Bill pulled the trigger and the tell-tale spark moved along the detonation wire towards the blasting caps.

Just then, Jack saw the divers coming for them. He pushed against Bill's arm and pointed frantically up and to their left. Bill saw them too. They both doused their lights and ducked behind large rock formations on the ledge and waited.

The two Colombian divers lost sight of their intended targets, but knew they were close to the rock opening that likely led into the treasure chamber. They thought they may have been spotted and stopped, hovering in the water waiting. They were looking for air bubbles escaping, as Bill and Jack exhaled.

Jack felt like he was a sitting duck and thought of a way to draw them in. He carefully pulled off his buoyancy control vest and placed it out away from him. He took a deep breath and released the regulator from his mouth. He kept the octopus safety air regulator near so he could take a quick puff of air as needed. The open regulator was spewing forth a ton of air bubbles that

Jack knew they could see coming up behind the rock formation, as if he was in distress. He pushed his vest further out. He didn't have to wait long.

One of the soldier/divers saw the vest and the bubbles coming up. He swam quickly over the rocks, and, zeroing in on the bubbles, fired his spear gun through the middle of Jack's vest which would have killed him. The diver's momentum carried him into close proximity of Jack's vest.

Jack knew they were in danger and he had planned this carefully. He quickly removed the safety cotter pin from the bang stick and waited. Suddenly the diver was floating past him looking at the vest. Out of the corner of his eye, he saw Jack approach, and tried to pull up and away but was too slow. With a mighty thrust, Jack jammed the end of the bang stick against his vest. There was a loud explosion, as the 12-gauge shotgun shell detonated against the man's chest killing him instantly! There was a huge recoil, which pushed Jack back against the rock formation. The octopus regulator flew out of his hand. For a few seconds, Jack frantically tried to find his buoyancy control device and his regulator, before he drowned. His weight belt held him down, but he knew if he released it, he would shoot to the surface too fast and would get the bends. Suddenly, he saw the bubbles still rising from his regulator, which had been pushed several feet away by the force of the spear. The enemy diver was laying on the sea floor, obviously dead. Jack swam to his vest and grabbed the octopus regulator, allowing his main regulator to continue to spew bubbles madly.

Suddenly, Jack saw the other diver coming at him from above and to his left. He was aiming another speargun at Jack and was about to fire. Jack twisted away, knowing it was too late! He suddenly heard another loud report, as Bill, from down below, and behind his own rock wall, reached up and shoved his bang stick into the other diver's chest, as he passed overhead. His charge detonated and also killed the soldier instantly, saving Jack from dying.

Bill frantically grabbed Jack's arm and tapped his watch with his dive knife. They had less than two minutes to get out of the Hole or they would be blown up! Jack put on what was left of his mostly destroyed buoyancy control life vest, fastened it around his waist and put his regulator back into his mouth. They both swam madly away from the rock formations, both knowing they would never make it out in time and would be killed by the blast.

Just then, Bill spotted the two dive scooters, which were neutrally buoyant, and were still floating at the same level as when they were stopped. Jack and Bill both swam frantically for them. They reached the scooters and grabbed them. They had push-button starters which fired up immediately. Bill indicated to Jack to stay behind him, as he would control the ascent. If they shot to the surface ahead of the explosion, they would die from the bends. If they stayed down too long, they would die from the explosion. Bill had to control this and he would be pushing the dive tables to the max!

Keeping his eye on his watch, he tried to time their ascent. He communicated to Miguel with his dive watch to drive the PT boat away from the Hole. They had power and would catch up. He said for them to get away by at least 1000 yards.

Dutifully, Miguel began to drive the PT boat away from the Hole over the protests of John, Kimmi and Manolo, who had no idea why he had suddenly fired up the PT boat and began to move it out and away from the Hole. Bill and Jack were on a diagonal course moving towards the PT boat, which was at a greater distance, but also kept them below the surface longer. Just as they broke the surface and saw the boat 500 yards away, the bomb detonated. There was a tremendous explosion and Bill and Jack were pushed along even faster by the pulsing wave!

Below the surface, the bomb Bill had placed caused the rock shelf the ship had rested on previously, to break free further and slide down the Hole, carrying the broken-up pirate ship to the bottom. A huge water plumb shot up through the hole over two hundred feet in the air!

Jack and Bill, covered their heads with one hand and accepted the fact that they would be propelled along the sea until they reached the boat.

They arrived at the PT boat in another five minutes, drenched and exhausted. Miguel had cut the power of the PT boat so they could catch up. Bill and Jack released the dive scooters, which floated away and down, as they chopped the power. Everyone reached into the water and helped them out, except Miguel, who was still at the helm and ready to resume driving the boat away from the explosion. They had a hard time getting the men onboard, as the PT boat rocked violently in the wake, caused by the detonation.

Bill and Jack sat on the deck, while the others helped pulled off their buoyancy control vests, tanks, fins and weight belts. They both took off their masks.

"How do you feel, Jack?" asked John.

"I'm OK. Pushed the tables a little too hard, but I'm OK."

"Bill?" John asked.

"Yeah, I'm OK too. Rough there at the end. Wonder what damage we did when we blew it up?"

John asked, "Why did you blow it?"

Bill smiled, "Because, mate, someone marked our spot with a giant white "X" over the entrance to the tunnel. And you know "X" should never mark the spot, but this time it did. And that's not good! So we blew it up!"

"Damnit," said John, "So now what? Sail to the island?"

"Yep," said Bill. No sense resting on our laurels. Let's go!" He got up, peeled off his wet suit, and went below to dry off and change. Jack did the same thing, while Miguel changed course to go to the island they had discussed earlier.

CHAPTER SEVEN

THE PIRATE'S ISLAND FORTRESS

ANGEL RAMERIEZ HAD WATCHED everything on the surface for the past half hour. Suddenly, he saw two divers break the surface of the water using his two water scooters, but they were not his men. They were dressed completely different. Then there was a huge explosion and he knew his men were dead and the tunnel, if there was one, was sealed off for good.

He slammed his fist into his open palm and spat on the deck. *You will pay for that dearly, my friend Bill Treese,* he thought. He kept watching the PT boat, which had changed course once the two divers had been picked up. It was turning back toward the island on his left. His first mate Tirrell was coming up the ladder.

"Captain," he said, "I think we lost our divers!"

"Yes," was Angel's short reply. "We are now focused on our mission at hand," Angel pointed out. "That island, it may be the end of the rainbow for us, with its pot of gold. If the PT boat is going there, so are we!"

Tirrell nodded, "Yes, sir."

"Plot a course to take us to the other side of the island. We will stay back and watch to see what happens, then land near the beach and take them all by surprise!"

Tirrell saluted him and made plans to get their boat underway.

****

The explosion in the water, near their island, drew the attention of Captain Lester Smith and the rest of his mates standing on the beach, near their huts, looking toward the sea.

"What the fuck?" said Trinidad, Blackbeard's first mate.

Blackbeard, also known as Captain Lester Smith, knew that whatever was happening was going to be a game changer. They saw the PT boat, that they had just engaged in battle the other day, racing away from the huge jettison of water that flew up over the Hole due to the underwater explosion.

He turned to his first mate Trinidad. "Where is our vessel?"

"In the cave, Captain."

Captain Lester grimaced. "OK, bring it out a little, so they can see it, but not too much. It looks like they are coming to us. They probably know the treasure is here on this island and they are looking for it. Place our men in the jungle and get them ready to board them when the time is right, *ya!*"

Everyone scrambled into position and Trinidad moved the vessel partly into the channel, so it could be identified, but not before it was too late.

****

Bill had taken over the controls. Manolo was on the Oerlikon cannon in the stern. Jack and John were on the twin .50s. Kimmi was next to Bill on the bridge. Miguel was down below, checking the engines and everything else that could go wrong.

Bill sailed quietly around the island. He had muffled the motors of the PT boat down to a quiet rumble. Stealth was desired, even though it was mid-morning and the Caribbean sun was up and already at a zenith. They could be spotted easily, but they continued anyway.

As they rounded the island, Bill spotted an inlet, which led back to a mountain, shaped like a volcano. He turned left and followed it back around a bend. It looked as though they were going straight into the mountain, but there was a cave up ahead and there was something just outside of it. Bill cut the power back even more.

They moved forward slowly, to see the air-sea rescue boat that they had fought earlier! *Bill thought for a second, what the fuck?* He came to a full stop, and allowed the heavy boat to drift slightly near the shore of the narrow passageway.

It was eerily quiet.

Suddenly, six pirates jumped onto the PT boat! They were armed with cutlasses and pulled Jack and John out of the twin machine gun turrets and dragged them out onto the deck. One pushed Bill down and pinned him there with his body. Another pirate grabbed Kimmi around the waist and pushed her down onto her back as she screamed. Manolo in the stern on the Oerlikon cannon ran forward, jumped on the day cabin roof, crossed it, and dove headfirst into the pirate holding her down in the bridge. He began beating the pirate with his fists over and over until his mate, holding Bill down, jumped up and kicked Manolo in his side savagely.

Bill used the opportunity to leap up. He reached into the console of the bridge for his Winchester rifle, but it had fallen down and he couldn't reach it! Next to his hand was his own sword, which was a Captain's sword from the American Civil War. He yanked it free and swung it at the pirate who had kicked Manolo. The pirate dove out of the way and Kimmi jumped up and ran over to help Manolo.

Bill was on the hunt and was ready to kill all six of the pirates. He charged two of them, who had fallen back towards the stern and was about to end their lives. He swung his sword over his head, bringing it down violently, only to be stopped by another sword, by a pirate who was hiding behind the day cabin. Their steel clashed savagely, and they both fell back! Bill regained his feet, jumped on the roof of the day cabin and looked back toward the stern.

A giant of a man stood up holding out his pirate's cutlass blade, which was similar to Bill's own Civil War sword, only a little fatter and a little shorter. Blackbeard the Pirate stood before Bill, all 6'5" of him, long black beard, dreadlocks, white pants, black boots, a rich red vest, with no shirt and a full black pirate's hat on. Just as in Bill's dreams!

An involuntary shudder went up Bill's spine, but he knew it was to kill or be killed!

The pirate smiled at Bill. Everyone else on the boat froze as he and Bill looked at each other.

"So, now you have nowhere to run this time, *mon!*" the pirate said to Bill. Bill smiled back at him. "Let's go, asshole! I have seen you in my dreams and am ready to end your fucking life!" Bill shouted as the pirate jumped onto the roof of the day cabin and their swords met with a thunderous crash.

Back and forth they swung their swords. There was no finesse, no subtle move, no attempt to stab, jab, parry, or thrust, just the fierce pounding of metal on metal, as sparks flew in every direction. Bill ducked as the pirate's sword passed over him and would have killed him, but it came dangerously close to Kimmi's head, who ducked down and screamed again. Manolo, in spite of the pain in his side from being kicked, jumped on top of her and held her down out of harm's way.

Bill realized he had to get off the boat or someone might be slashed inadvertently.

Suddenly he leaped off the day cabin onto the deck and jumped off the boat onto the sand.

The pirate roared with laughter, "Run, *mon*, run, but you can't hide on *I and I's* island!"

Bill turned around and yelled, "No one's hiding from you, bitch! Come on, fucker! You dress like a pirate, but you look like a pussy to me!" He gestured with his arms for the pirate to join him on the sand. "Fight to the end!"

With a roar, knowing he had finally found the true adversary he had always dreamed of, Captain Lester Smith leaped off the day cabin, onto the deck and then jumped down to the beach.

Bill had backed up to give him room. Both men held out

their swords and began circling each other. No one on the PT boat dared to move. They were all watching this battle in awe. Captain Lester, glanced back at his men, including his first mate Trinidad, who was watching and holding his own cutlass.

"No one is to interfere, *mon!*" Lester yelled back at Trinidad, "This is to the death!"

He looked at Bill, "To the death, my friend!"

Bill nodded, "To the end!"

At that moment, they both came at each other with a mighty crash of their swords. They battled for over a minute. The steel flew in the morning sun, partially blinding the two crews on the PT boat. Both Bill and Lester neither giving an inch, were beginning to tire. Bill was working his way to the side of the pirate and kept hacking towards his right arm. Bill was moving closer and closer to him. This was dangerous, but Bill had a plan. The pirate kept swinging his cutlass to the right and parrying off Bill's advances. Suddenly, Bill, swinging shorter and shorter, stuck his right leg behind the pirate's right leg and shoved him with his sword. The move caught Captain Lester by surprise and he flew backwards and landed on his back, still clutching his sword. Bill leapt on top of him and with three quick swings knocked the sword out of the pirate's hand! Bill pressed his sword against the pirate's neck. They stared at each other.

Trinidad, seeing his captain and boyhood friend about to be killed, jumped off the PT boat and began to run at them screaming. Lester looked up and yelled at his friend, "Belay that, *mon*, stay right the fuck there!! *This mon wanna go to Heaven, but he no wanna die, either!*" The Jamaican pirate threw back his head and howled with laughter.

Trinidad froze on the sand halfway there, did not put down his cutlass, but held it out menacingly at Bill, who was standing over the pirate.

Bill and the pirate were both panting and sweating furiously in the heat. Bill increased the pressure of his sword against the pirate's throat. "Do you yield? Do you yield?" said Bill, who did not want to kill him in cold blood now that he was vanquished, but hoped there might be an alternative.

The pirate stopped laughing, "No, *mon*, kill me if ye dare, but there will be a thousand curses upon you if you do!"

"I've already been cursed, twice in fact, and I'm going to die because of pirates like you and their cursed treasure!"

"Do it, *mon*, do it!" Lester shouted at Bill.

"May I have your name, sir, before I run you through?"

Once again the pirate threw back his head and laughed out loud. "Blackbeard! I am Blackbeard the Pirate!"

"What is you birth name, Blackbeard?" shouted Bill, "I demand it!"

The pirate moved up on his elbows in the sand and looked Bill directly in the eye. I am Captain Lester Smith!" he yelled out loudly.

John, Jack, Kimmi and Manolo let out a collective gasp. Bill's eyes widened. "Did you say Lester Smith?"

Ya, *mon*, I don't stutter, Fuck Head!" he screamed at Bill.

Slowly Bill backed off, from where he was straddling him. He raised his sword above his head. Everyone gasped and held their breath. Bill brought his sword down with all the force and furry in his being. The tip of the sword crashed into the sand next to the head of the pirate, burying it half way to the hilt, where it wobbled back and forth! Bill, letting go of his sword, stepped to the side of Lester Smith and held out his hand.

Lester, not understanding what had just happened, put his hand up and took Bill's outstretched hand. He pulled him up off of the sand. They looked each other in the eye.

"Captain Lester Smith, I'm not going to kill you today. I have something of great value, which belongs to you. It is in the hold of my vessel. May I send two of my crew down below to get it?"

Lester, looked at Bill with shock and surprise. "Yes," he said quietly.

Bill yelled out, "Manolo, you and Miguel bring up the chest!

Manolo went below to find Miguel, who had been waiting below with his AR-15 assault rifle, looking for a chance to come up and help his mates. Instead, he and Manolo grabbed the treasure chest and hauled it up the ladder. The pirate's eyes on board the PT boat widened, as they had never really seen an actual pirate's treasure chest.

Manolo lowered the gangplank to the sand and they carried the heavy chest between them, past Trinidad and placed it at the feet of Lester Smith.

Bill stepped back and said, "I believe this belongs to you. It is a gift from a relative of yours. A gift to you and the lifting of a curse from me," he looked over at his boat, "and my mates."

Lester got on his knees and opened the lid of the chest. Looking inside, he smiled. On top was the letter from his great grandfather, Captain Lester Smith. He picked up the paper and read the inscription. He glanced at Bill, "Mi great grandpa, ya!"

He set the note in the sand and pulled back the oilskin and the heavy red cloth. His breath caught in his throat as he looked at the six daggers and the gold bars inside. He pulled out one of the swords and read the inscription on the blade.

He looked at Bill and smiled, pointing the weapon at Bill, "You would have been cursed, *mon*. Lucky I come along to save YOU!" He threw back his head and laughed. He yelled for his crew to come and look. They all jumped off the boat and ran over to their captain. They gathered around as Lester handed the swords to them and also the heavy gold bars. Jack, Kimmi and John joined them as the pirates yelled happily at the discovery.

Bill looked over at Miguel. "Hey, Miguel, can you bring me a canteen of water, please? I'm dying of thirst right now." Miguel nodded and jumped up and ran to the boat. Once there, he realized Bill's canteen on the bridge was empty, so he went below to fill it with cool water.

Bill came up to Lester and patted him on the shoulder. Lester, standing up, towered over Bill by at least four inches. "So was Captain Lester Smith your great grandfather?"

"Ya, *mon*. He tricked the American Union soldiers, who were going to hang him. This treasure is in my family name. Where did you find it, ya?"

"Well, the first three swords in the Blue Hole on a sunken ship, that we were lucky to have discovered. It was resting on a ledge about 70 feet down."

"Yes!" Lester's head was bobbing madly up and down with excitement, "That was his ship, mon! It was shot out from under him and it sank. There still?"

Bill shook his head, "No, parts of it might be, but we had

to blow the ledge it was sitting on, and it probably broke up and crashed down to the bottom of the Hole."

"Why did you blow it up, *mon?*"

"Because we didn't want anyone to find the entrance to the tunnel that branched off from it."

Lester's eyes went wide and he grabbed Bill by both shoulders. "Did you explore the tunnel, *mon?*"

Bill smiled and nodded, "I think I have something else to show you…"

Suddenly, there were bullets flying over their heads and six men were running at them from the opposite end of the beach.

"Don't anyone move," one of them shouted, "or you will all be dead!" The pirates looked at Captain Lester and the others looked at Bill. None of them had any weapons, other than Bill and Lester's swords, lying uselessly in the sand.

The men stopped running a few yards from them. Angel Rameriez held up an AK-47 and aimed it at Bill and the big pirate. "Well, Bill Treese, we meet again! I see you have met the legendary Blackbeard the Pirate! The notorious bushwhacker of the Caribbean! I hear there is a price on his head, dead or alive! That will be my pleasure to collect along with the legendary treasure chamber that belonged to his great grandaddy! I have no doubt you have found that and," he gestured towards the chest, "a little something extra!"

"Who the fuck is this *jabbermon?*" asked Lester.

Bill spoke up, "His name is Angel and he thinks he is some kind of playboy treasure hunter, but he is a pimp and an amateur!"

Angel held his rifle up and advanced toward Bill, who did not flinch, but stood his ground.

"My trigger finger is itchy and needs to be scratched," Angel smiled, "But not yet." He lowered the gun to his side. "Plenty of time for fun and games in a minute. So, where's the treasure? Not these trinkets."

"Oh," said Bill, "they're not trinkets. I'd say each sword is worth a hundred thousand, and there are six of them. You should read the inscription on them!" Angel motioned for one of his men to pick up the dagger, who handed it to him. Angel held it up to the light so he could read the inscriptions on it. He could only understand the part that was written in Spanish, but not the other symbols. He suddenly dropped it in the sand and kicked it back towards the group. "So now I am supposed to be cursed! Well, what if I tell you I don't believe in curses and you can keep your little daggers and bring them when you march into hell in a few minutes!"

Angel turned to his men, "Lead them over to the base of the mountain. We will see who is really cursed and who will live through this!"

CHAPTER EIGHT

THE FLIGHT OF THE U.S. NAVY

ON BOARD THE PT BOAT, MIGUEL HAD finished pouring water into Bill's canteen, when he heard the gunfire and the commotion coming from the beach. He dropped the canteen and quickly ascended the ladder to the deck. He looked over the side of the PT boat and saw the men on the beach holding their weapons at Bill, his crew and the pirates. He started to go back and get his own rifle, but then realized he couldn't get close enough to get a clear shot. He would likely be cut to pieces by the other men, who looked like professional soldiers. *He thought, what would Capitain Bill do?* So he went back into the charthouse and, taking out the microphone off its stand on the radio, began reading from an emergency note on the wall.

"Mayday, mayday, any ship come in. Peter Tare, Peter Tare in trouble. Armed men are here and are going to shoot us! Peter Tare in trouble. Coordinates are," he looked up at the red sonar readings that told their position and

said them. He repeated this phrase over and over again.

Five hundred miles away, the USS Carl Vinson aircraft carrier was patrolling the eastern Caribbean Sea. Captain Bryce Wong and Commander Josh Covington (call sign "Batman" because of his high, tight, G Force change of headings like the Batmobile), were drinking coffee and standing in the Command Information Center, otherwise known as the CIC, when the call came through from the PT boat.

"Say again, say again, Peter Tare, say again!" the radio officer said into his mike. The distress call was made again.

The radioman looked over at Captain Rush, who was concentrating on a set of orders he was reading through. "Captain, sir, I don't know what they are talking about, or what they are saying. It makes no sense to me, sir!"

The captain looked up, "OK, put it on speaker phone." He looked around the room, snapping his fingers.

"Listen up people!"

Miguel's voice suddenly filled the room, ***"Mayday, mayday, any ship come in. Peter Tare, Peter Tare in trouble. Armed men are here and are going to shoot us! Peter Tare in trouble. Coordinates are as follows."***

Captain Rush looked around the room. "Anyone know what the hell Peter Tare means?"

Captain Wong said, "Yes sir, I do! Remember that wild tale I told you about me being rescued by Americans on a PT boat? Well, sir, that is them! I'm sure of it! That is the name the Australian Coast Watchers identified the PT boats by during World War II because they knew the Japanese Navy was listening to their transmissions." He looked at the radio officer. "What are those coordinates?"

He told him and Captain Wong said to the Captain, "Sir, they are only 500 miles away! Permission to take the F-35C Lightning II and help them, sir? Please, sir. They saved my life!"

The Captain nodded. They were allowed to go into battle to protect American lives and that is what he would put in his captain's log book. "Ok." He looked at Commander Covington and shook his head as if in dismay. "Take this sorry sack of a sailor as your wingman, too, please! I would like to see him do some work for a change!" He rolled his eyes, as Covington laughed and set down his coffee. "Yes sir!" Commander Covington saluted him. They both took off for the flight deck, running out of the CIC and down the ladders as fast as they could.

Miguel, still sending out the distress signal, was about to give up when his radio cracked to life,

"Rodger that, Peter Tare! This is the USS Carl Vinson. F-35C Lightning II on the way to intercept at your coordinates. Buy us a couple of minutes if you can! The music is coming, take precaution! Good luck, sailor! We're with you and we're out!"

Miguel took a deep breath and said a quick prayer. The only way he could buy them time is if he engaged the enemy. But all he had was his AR-15 assault rifle, which was only one gun against many. He knew he had to try. He slung his rifle over his shoulder, grabbed his helmet and survival knife, and headed up the ladder.

Miguel reached the deck and laid down, holding his rifle to his side. They were about 50 yards away from him, but at a terrible angle for him to engage combat. His crew, *Capitian* Bill, Manolo, Jack, John and Kimmi were next to the side of the mountain. The pirates also had their backs against the mountain. *Capitain* Bill was standing next to the big pirate named Lester.

The four mercenaries, the man in command named Angel and his first mate, Tirrell, were talking loudly and fast to their prisoners. As best as Miguel could make out, they were demanding they show them to the hidden treasure chamber, which his crew had found earlier. But he knew *Capitain* Bill would never tell them anything.

Miguel could see the man, Angel, who had approached them before on his yacht a few days ago, was getting more and more angry. He was strutting around screaming at them to tell him where the treasure was. Miguel brought his rifle up to the deck rail and aimed it. If Angel moved into his sights, he would be the first Miguel would shoot and, then the rest would have to take care of itself.

On the deck of the U.S.S. Carl Vinson, Captain Bryce Wong and Commander Josh Covington were being strapped into their respective aircrafts, the F-35C Lightning II jets which could take off and land vertically, but were being prepared for a short horizontal take off to conserve fuel. Both pilots knew their aircraft were extremely difficult to fly and were considered to be unforgivable if they made a mistake.

They took off with the catapults used for the fixed wing aircraft and were soon in the sky. Captain Wong punched in the coordinates he had been given. He pressed his accelerator forward and leveled his elevators. His thruster shot him forward, as Commander Covington followed him.

Streaking towards their target, Captain Wong realized they were about to become supersonic, and just as he thought this, both pilots head the sonic boom associated with blowing through the speed barrier!

Those on the island 200 miles away, heard the sonic boom, but did not know what it meant.

Bill Treese, looking up at the sky whispered to Captain Lester, "The good guys are on their way."

Lester looked up, "What guys, *mon?*"

Suddenly, Angel appeared in front of them and hit them both across their heads with his pistol. "Enough talk, you bastards!"

Lester started to jump up and Bill reached out to him, by grabbing his arm. He shook his head, as if to say no, save it for later.

Lester seethed and was dying to take his revenge on this stupid, fluffy fat man.

Angel, with two of his men, kicked Lester and Bill in their backs, causing them to fall to their knees. He reached out, as his men placed their rifle barrels into the ribs of their two captives. "Speak of the gold. Where is it? It is on this island! I know it! There is a tunnel between here and the Blue Hole that hides it! Where is it?!" He slapped Bill on the back of his head. Bill fell face first onto the sand. He did not move or try to fight back. He made himself look helpless.

Angel kicked Bill in the side, which raised Bill up off of the sand. Bill again appeared helpless. Angel screamed at him, "Where is it? I know you know!" He yelled at his men. "Bind them all. Set them back against the mountain. The firing squad begins!"

Suddenly, his men began binding everyone with some thin rope, which was not the best deterrent because it was loose and too sloppy. But it was all they had.

Most of them protested. Jack was clubbed across the back of his head. The pirates all tried to fight back and were hit over and over again, until they were compliant. John and Manolo fought back until they were also hit on the back of their heads. Kimmi backed up as two of the soldiers tried to rip her shirt off and grab her chest. Angel saw this and screamed at them in Spanish to leave her alone and to tie her up. There was no time for this foolishness!

Angel yelled at his men to pull them all back to the mountain base and stand them up. He was going to end this once and for all. He grabbed Bill by the collar. "One last chance to end this!" he shouted, "Where is the entrance to the cave?" He slapped Bill across his mouth, drawing blood and causing Bill to fall back onto the sand.

Bill smiled up at him, "Find it your own fucking self, " he grinned.

This caused Angel to go into an outrage. He began kicking Bill in the side over and over until his first mate, Tirrell ran over and pushed him back.

"Jeeze, Captain, you really hurt him," as Bill rolled on the sand coughing up blood. For once Bill Treese was at the mercy of his enemies. He did not have a sword, or a gun or even a back up plan. For the first time he was vulnerable and could die at any moment.

Bill smiled to himself, *Oh, well, it's been a hell of a ride, but it has to end sometime. He smiled. He was ok. This pussy couldn't kick his way out of a wet paper bag.*

Angel ran over to a white cotton bag he had laid in the sand. He reached inside and, with one hand, grabbed a handful of white powder and inhaled it through his nose. Bill and Lester, looking up, thought this was probably pure cocaine, he was stuffing up his nose. They both decided that this was an advantage.

Angel yelled at his men, "Line 'em up. We're going to execute these *hombres!*

His men pushed everyone back to the mountain.

Miguel, on the PT boat, saw them being pushed back and knew they were about to be shot by Angel and his men. He decided to take action, even though it might not be the right action and could get everyone killed. He took careful aim at Angel and prepared to shoot.

****

Captain Wong and Commander Covington were both still flying toward the island and were starting their descent. With their F-35C Lightning II jets screaming, they pointed their noses down towards the pirate's island. Captain Wong was in the lead, and Commander Covington was off his right wing. Their instruments told them they would be at the island in 75 seconds. They began to slow their descent immediately, so that they could appraise the situation and, if need be, get off a clear shot at any hostilities they might see. Since they had been traveling at almost 600 knots, they would fly straight into the ground if they did not slow up.

****

Angel was in his moment. It was true he did not have the cave, only a small treasure chest. But he was confident that, with his ground piercing sonar equipment, he could find the lost tunnel, which would lead back to the chamber, that held the treasure. Ever since Tirrell had spoken about the likelihood of them finding the long-lost treasure from the 1800's pirate's plunder, he had been excited as he thought about the possibilities. With that kind of money, he could buy a whole country and fortify it with his own army and navy! He could wreak havoc around the islands and plunder them for treasure, drugs, women or anything else he could imagine. He knew Bill wouldn't tell him anything, and the stupid pirate probably had no idea where the entrance was. If he had, he would have already collected it and gotten away from here. He sure as hell would not have let Bill stay alive! That would have been his first order of business.

Angel smiled. It was time to teach these *gringos* a little lesson in respect and diplomacy. In other words, who was the Big Boss around here.

He yelled at his men to assume the position to open fire on these *gringos.*

Bill and his crew knew this was inevitable. John jumped up and begged them to spare his daughter. Angel, after looking over Kimmi, said, "She's too skinny for me!" and laughed. "Kill her along with the rest!" he shouted to his men, who were about to raise their rifles.

Angel yelled out on my mark! "Ready, set," but before he could get to aim and fire, the air and the island shook with the sound of jet engines as the jets came screaming down on them!

Miguel, on the PT boat, who was about to squeeze the trigger and kill Angel, stopped, but kept his gun trained on his intended target.

Captain Wong saw immediately what was happening. He recognized the crew of the PT boat that had rescued him, along with several others, pushed back against the cliff, as though they were being executed by a firing squad. He took one second to make a decision. He pushed his aircraft further into the "nose down" position and, aiming for the men who held the rifles, opened up on them with all the fury he could muster with his machine gun bullets.

Angel's four men and his first mate, Tirrell, were cut down immediately by the F-35C Lightning II, as Angel, who was standing off to the side, dove out of the way. Everyone else ducked for cover behind the rocks, as Captain Wong pulled up and flew upward. Commander Covington, Captain Wong's wingman followed him, but did not fire.

With pure hate, Angel fired his AK-47 at the escaping jets. *Where the hell had these planes come from*, he thought. Firing at them was a useless gesture, even as both planes returned and, using their thrusters, landed on the beach. They landed next to each other facing Angel on the beach, who still held his weapon and began to fire on the planes in a wild attempt to stop them. Not wishing to kill him, Commander Covington fired a volley of bullets over Angel's head. He used his speaker to yell out at Angel, "Drop your weapon now!" Angel, realizing his situation was hopeless, dropped his rifle on the sand. Bill and the others popped their heads up behind the rocks. They realized they were safe, as they looked at Angel's dead soldiers lying in the sand.

Captain Wong popped open the canopy of his aircraft. He stood up and pointed his sidearm hand gun, in this case it was a Beretta M9. He shouted out to Angel, "Sir! You are my prisoner!"

"Fuck that!" Angel screamed at him and suddenly ran over to the rocks, which were on the edge of the water, just past the beach. His boat was floating only a few yards away, and the water beyond the rocks was at least twenty feet deep. The pure cocaine he had been stuffing up his nose, had affected his judgment. He thought he could swim to his boat and shove off. Even if he were to be cut down by these Navy jets, he could still make a run for it and possibly shoot at least one of them out of the sky!

He jumped up on the top rock and screaming hysterically, pulled out his own handgun, a Sig Sauer model 1911 .45 ACP semi auto pistol and began firing wildly at the planes, Bill, Lester and their crews. Everyone dove again for cover, as the bullets came dangerously close. Captain Wong was forced to duck below his canopy as a bullet flew past his head.

Suddenly, Miguel, still lying on the deck of the PT boat, aimed at Angel and fired a shot, which went directly through his heart. Angel screamed and fell backwards, dead, into the water. He floated for a few seconds. In a matter of moments, three tiger sharks, who had smelled blood, swam in and began to tear his body apart.

Captain Wong jumped out of his aircraft and started to point his gun at Miguel, who jumped up and dropped his rifle on the deck of the PT boat with a loud clatter. He raised his hands over his head in surrender.

"Captain Wong," Bill shouted from behind the rocks, "he's

with me!"

Captain Wong placed his sidearm back in its holster. He looked at Bill, "I knew that!" he said.

Commander Covington got out of his jet and jumped down on the beach. Bill, Jack, Kimmi, John, Manolo, Lester, Trinidad and the rest of the pirates came out from behind the rocks, which were next to the mountain. Miguel ran down the gangplank and joined them all on the sand. He began to quickly take off everyone's rope bindings, setting them all free.

Captain Wong took command. He walked over to Bill and, against protocol, embraced him. "I told you I owed you!" he said.

Bill nodded, "Your timing on paying your debt to me was excellent," he said. "I told you that you didn't owe me anything, but I am very glad you ignored me!" They all laughed, as much at the joke, but more so out of relief that they had not been shot by Angel's firing squad.

Captain Wong looked around. "I know your crew, Bill, but who are these other, should I say, pirates?" Captain Lester started to speak up, but Bill cut him off.

"Captain Wong, United State Navy, this is Captain Lester. He owns this island, and it was our good fortune to land here to bring him greetings and good times, before our mercenary friends showed up and tried to kill us."

Captain Wong was looking at Lester closely. "OK, so who was the leader of the mercenaries?" asked Captain Wong."

Bill spoke up again, "Have you ever heard of Blackbeard the Pirate?"

"Of course, I have! There is a price on his head down

here. Are you saying the man that attacked you, tried to execute you, tried to kill me and then was shot by your own man was Blackbeard the Pirate?"

Bill nodded slowly.

Captain Wong was no fool. He was staring straight at Captain Lester. "I had heard that Blackbeard the Pirate was a Jamaican with long dreads and a long black beard, usually dressed like a pirate."

Bill nodded again, "You know, I heard that too, and I think it is a case of mistaken identity!" He smiled.

Captain Wong looked from Bill to Lester and back again. "Well that guy looked Latin and he was cleanshaven. I guess we can go over and drag his body up for a closer look." Bill suddenly looked worried.

Captain Wong turned to Commander Covington, "Commander, can you please go see if his body is floating by the rocks?"

"Certainly sir!"

He walked over to the rocks near the water and climbed up. Looking down, he yelled back, "Uh, no sign of him, sir, but there are three big sharks swimming around and a lot of blood in the water."

Captain Wong looked back up at Bill, who was smiling again. "Well, Bill, how convenient." He looked back at Captain Lester, and shook his head. "I'm not sure how I am going to write this up in my log, but I am sure I will have to be creative!" He looked at the dead soldiers on the beach he had killed. "Do you want me to send over a Navy helicopter, with a crew to clean up this mess? I assume since they were about to shoot all of you, that you will identify them to the local authorities and give them a proper burial."

Bill nodded, "I think we can handle it from here. You both have been very helpful and have saved our lives. No need to send the Navy out. We will file the necessary papers, report to the authorities that Blackbeard and his crew are dead and there will be no more pirating activities from this quarter." Bill reached out his hand, "Thank you again, Captain Wong, and I still remember that offer to bring my PT boat to Pearl Harbor for a visit with the Navy!" Bill stepped back and saluted Captain Wong, who returned his salute.

Commander Covington was walking up to his plane and Captain Wong walked over to him. "How the hell are we going to write this up?" asked Commander Covington.

"Just like it happened. We were part of a rescue mission, to help out fellow Americans, who were about to be executed by Blackbeard the Pirate. In the exchange of gunfire, Blackbeard and his crew were unfortunately killed."

Commander Covington smiled, "Yes, sir!"

Captain Wong said, "OK. Let's return to our ship."

He turned and waved to Bill, Lester and their crewmen. He and Commander Covington climbed back into their respective cockpits, as everyone moved away, to stay away from the blast of the jet engines. Both planes fired up and began to take off vertically. When they had reached a height of two hundred feet, they both turned in the direction of their mother ship and flew away into the late morning sky.

CHAPTER NINE
THE TREASURE OF CAPTAIN LESTER SMITH

CAPTAIN LESTER SMITH TURNED TO BILL AND laughed, "You were lying your ass off, *mon!* But thank you!"

Bill smiled, "You're welcome! Now I have something important to show you! But before I do that, if I showed you something fantastic that would change your life forever, and would make you and your crew wealthier than you ever dreamed of, would you kill me and my crew, and return to pirating, or would you quit and do something good?"

Lester smiled, "Do you know why we were pirating, *mon*, other than I was born into it by mi father and mi mother?"

"No," said Bill.

"To start a school in Jamaican, *mon*, like mi grandpa and grandma, who were not pirates. They were school teachers and the people of Jamaica need schools, where the children can play and be educated. They have some in the cities, but nothing in the country where good boys and girls may become bad because they can't read or write. That is my mission, *mon*, not piratin'. That was a means to an end. We never killed no one. Just took money from the fluffy rich white boys out here!"

"Good," said Bill. "That's what I was hoping to hear. Now let's be on our way!"

Captain Lester's heart skipped a beat. In a whisper, he said, "Show me."

Bill turned and said to the group, "Everyone needs to see this!"

Bill led the party over, past the cave that held the air-sea rescue boat, past the huts and stopped at the base of the mountain, where the vines covered the opening to the secret tunnel.

He reached into his belt and pulled out his military Ka-Bar knife and began cutting away the heavy vines. They fell to the ground and the group was staring at what appeared to be simply the rocky side of the mountain.

Lester looked perplexed, "What is it, *mon?*" he asked.

Bill reached above his head and, finding the other side of the crack, that he and Jack had looked out from the other day, pressed his knife into the crack and pushed it down through the heavy mud that had sealed off the rock from the entrance to the tunnel for over 150 years. He was able to cut and saw away until he reached the base on the left of the rocks. Bill then went back to the top of the entrance and began doing the same thing to the right side, until he reached the ground.

He stepped back and turned to Captain Lester. "Like I said, I have something to show you, I just hope it's all still there and not underwater." Bill began to push against one side of the rock-way blocking the tunnel. To his surprise, it swung inward easily, and as they discovered, it was heavy, but pivoted on a large hinge system.

Bill stepped back and looked at Lester, whose eyes were wide open, as if in shock. "My God, *mon*, is that what I think it is?"

Bill smiled, "Well I hope it is!" He turned to Manolo and Miguel, "Can you two run to the ship and get some flashlights, please?" They both took off. Miguel was especially excited because he had not seen the treasure yet.

Lester, looking around, slapped his forehead with his hands. "We've been coming here since I was a boy, looking for this and it was right here all along." He slapped his forehead again, "If it were a snake, it would have bit me!"

Bill smiled and asked, "Captain Lester, do you have any lanterns? It's kind of dark down there." Lester turned to his men and without saying anything, two of them ran back to the huts and brought back four electric lanterns. By then Manolo and Miguel had also joined them.

Bill took a step inside the tunnel. He turned to Lester, who had to duck down because of his height. "Good sign," said Bill.

"What's that?" Lester asked.

"It's dry so far," said Bill

Behind Lester, came John, Jack, Kimmi, Manolo and Miguel. Behind them, was Trinidad and the rest of Lester's crew.

As they descended, Bill carefully made his way forward. Using the flashlight, he looked for signs of water, but there wasn't any. He had butterflies in his stomach, praying that Angel had not somehow stolen the treasure. But, by the way Angel had been screaming at them before his sad demise, he doubted it. But if it wasn't there, he did not doubt Captain Lester Smith would shoot him immediately and his crew too.

As he prepared to make the last turn, he took a deep breath and looked into the treasure chamber. He breathed a sigh of relief. The floor was wet, probably from the explosion. He walked in, holding his flashlight. Lester came in and held up his lantern. The breath caught in his throat and he was speechless as he looked at the enormous amount of treasure that was in front of him.

"Trinidad, Trinidad, come look! It's our salvation, *mon!*"

By then everyone was in the treasure chamber and were all astonished by the sheer amount of wealth.

Bill said, "Take a look around. I am pretty sure it all belonged to your great grandfather! Many years of staying neutral in a war, but attacking both sides, has its rewards!"

"Ya, *mon*, but he was trying to do a good *ting*, helping them Union boys out and they betray his good intentions. They get what's coming to them, ya!"

Bill smiled, "That's probably a good story. Maybe we can discuss it over dinner tonight. Uh, can we get a small finder's fee for all of this?"

Lester threw back his head and laughed, "Of course, *mon!* Fifty/fifty right down the middle!"

Bill laughed, "Very generous, but I think you're going to need a lot of this for that school you want to build. I was hoping for maybe around 10 percent, but it doesn't have to be tallied up and weighed, like we are lawyers. Whatever you can give us to help us replace our hard costs and the ordinance we had to use."

Lester looked at Bill suddenly and cocked an eye at him, "So you want me to pay you for the torpedo you shot at me?"

Bill looked away, sheepishly, "Uh, well I wasn't going to put it quite like that, but yes, as a matter of fact!"

Everybody laughed and Lester put his arm around Bill. "Whatever you say, *mon*, you have changed our lives right now!" He turned to his crew, "What say ye boys! Shall we trade our swords for books and chalkboards?"

"Aye, Captain!" they all said.

Lester said, "This is a great day! Can we look around, *mon?* This is a great day!" he said again.

"Of course," said Bill. "It is your treasure! Your inheritance!"

John spoke up, "Captain Lester, I am Professor John Waales. I am an archaeologist from U.C. Berkeley in California. With your permission, I would like to help you catalogue all of this, and maybe my daughter, Kimmi and I could help you set up your school. I have many years of teaching under my belt. It's up to you of course."

Lester smiled and reached out his hand. You would be most welcome, Professor." He looked around. Mi men and I don't quite know where to begin!"

Bill said, "Well, to begin with, I think you're going to need a cargo vessel to haul this treasure away! Second, you will have to figure out what to do with it, keep some, sell some; will the government want part of it? Lots of questions."

Lester nodded. He looked over at Trinidad, "For now, the less people know about this, the better, ya," said Lester.

After that, everyone walked around to admire the hordes of treasure. Lester stopped at the bed and looked up at the painting of the pirate, "Mi great grandpa," he said as Jack walked over. All of them had made formal introductions earlier.

"Yes," Jack said, "I am sure of it." Jack looked over at the night stand. He walked up to it and picked up one of the flint-lock pistols. He carefully handed it to Lester. "These guns have your great grandfather's name on them, but be careful, I don't know if they are loaded or not."

Lester held it in his hands and looked over it, "This is amazing, *mon*. Like a museum under the ocean!" It matches what I heard about him!"

Jack nodded, "Will you really use all of this to build a school in Jamaica?" he asked.

Lester turned to look at him and smiled, "Ya, *mon!* It is what I and I want. To help the little ones turn out good and also to help the bad ones, to turn out better. I think mi and mi mates can straighten out even the toughest lads! Ha ha! Nobody, wants to mess around with a pirate, especially a teenager! In six months, you will come to Jamaica and see it! To celebrate with us, ya!"

Jack smiled, "That's a deal! Can I bring my wife, Lisa? We had our honeymoon in Negril, but that was a long time ago."

Lester put out his hand and shook Jack's hand. "It would be my honor, to welcome you and your bride to mi island and see mi school!"

Jack said, "That is a deal!"

As the afternoon grew longer, Lester sent two of his men to make lunch for them and their guests. He also sent them to do a grim but necessary task. They had to do double duty, as they collected and tossed the bodies of Angel's soldiers into the same shark-infested pool that Angel had fallen in. They got the soldier's weapons, took a small powered inflatable boat out to Angel's yacht and sailed it into the cave. They went through it and found the money his men had gotten for the drugs they had found on the sunken ship and brought it back to shore. Later, they would likely take the boat out to sea and scuttle it in deep water. It depended on what Captain Lester wanted to do. Then they went to their land kitchen and prepared a large meal of fish, papaya, mangos, rice and other local fruit.

Two hours later, they were all seated around a big table, feasting on the late lunch. They made their plans, Bill, Jack, Manolo, Miguel, Kimmi and John would stay for a few days to help them bring out the gold to the huts. Trinidad had an uncle, who would lend them one of his small cargo ships, which they could use for the foreseeable future. Lester had a home in the country, not too far from Kingston. It was there most of the gold would be taken. Lester also had an uncle, who was a banker and could help them turn some of the gold into paper assets, such as stocks and bonds. Lester also had an interest in real estate, especially buying up properties in the slum areas of Kingston and refurbishing them.

Bill had a question for Lester, but he wanted to word it carefully. "Captain Lester," he said, "I have a question, but I want to be careful how I ask it."

"Ask away, *mon.* After all we have been through?" he laughed.

"OK. Those swords and the messages he left in the treasure chests," Bill cleared his throat loudly, "Was your great grandfather a devil worshiper, who really leveled curses on anyone who found his treasure, and especially those swords?"

Lester looked over at Bill and smiled broadly, "Ha ha! No

mon! Those were meant for anyone outside mi family! We knew they were only a warning! It was in his diary, that he left us. He was a good Christian man, who believed in good and helped everyone he could! He did big *tings, mon!* He was a *rad man!"*

"So there never was a real curse?" asked Bill incredulously.

Lester smiled again, "There was if you believed in one! Many a good man has died in these waters because he took the curse on himself and believed in it! Ha ha!"

Bill lowered his head and smiled. "Faked out again! Damn! So, you really didn't save me from anything!"

"Ya, *mon,* I saved you from yourself and your crew too! You believed in it and it would have haunted you until you found ME! And that was your salvation!"

Lester was silent for a minute. "But it didn't help that poor bastard we fed to the fishes today! Ha, ha! He'll burn in hell for it, while he dances with the devil!"

Bill nodded.

They continued to eat in silence for a while, thinking about Angel and his crew.

Wanting to lighten up the conversation, Bill turned again to Lester whose mouth was full of fish and rice. He said, "You have big plans, my friend. It could take you a lifetime!"

Lester nodded, "Ya, but what a difference we could make in the lives of our countrymen! People aren't bad, *mon,* but grow up in a bad way and make hard choices. We can help a lot of people with what you have delivered us to today."

"That's good," Bill said. "It'll take a while to build a school from the ground up, won't it?

Lester smiled, "Not necessary. There is a large campus

near my home that closed. No money there. Sad. Nice place. I know the government would give it to mi for good price and approve our charter. Maybe a small gift here and there of gold to them. They like gifts. Most politicians do. Not greed, mon, just the way to lubricate the system, like a boat or a woman, ya!" he smiled.

"Will you bring in Professor Waales to help you?"

"Oh, that is a gift for us. An American professor from your U.C. Berkeley? Helping us to create a school? That is *rad*, mon. He can help us with the treasure. If there are masterpieces of jewelry, medallions, and the like, he can help us establish a providence. Maybe set up a museum or a library, where others can enjoy. Maybe a museum for mi great grandpa that would honor his name and tell of his great deeds!" He looked away, his eyes getting misty, "That would be bomb, *mon*."

Bill smiled, "Thank goodness I didn't kill you on the beach today. Look what we would have missed!"

Lester gave him a sideways glance, "I was just resting for the moment, ya. I had you right where I wanted you!"

They both laughed and returned to their food.

The next two days were busy, as they brought everything up from the treasure cave. John took inventory and catalogued the treasure as best as he could. There was a lot that he had no idea what it was, but would take time and, possibly later down the road, work with some of the local archaeologists on Jamaica, to see what they actually had. Rare antiquities would likely be loaned to the government for the public to enjoy. They knew the story would get out, but they wanted to control as much of it as possible.

Lester was surprised by the cash his men had discovered on Angel's yacht. One point two million dollars was a lot of money. He told his men they could each have $200,000, but to hide the money and not tell anyone in the government where they got it. To spend it wisely and carefully when they got home.

By the end of the third day, the small cargo ship had arrived. The captain was Trinidad's uncle, who, in spite of being the head of his company with over a dozen ships and two hundred employees, wanted to see this one badly. He did not even bring a mate because he knew this had to be kept quiet. This was going to be a very big deal and would help all of them in the future. It took a full day to get everything onto the ship. The hold was filled and then locked down. They would sail to Jamaica, with Lester on the air-sea boat following behind. Angel's yacht was deemed too valuable to scuttle, so two of Lester's crew spent a day changing the name, numbers and anything else that would help identify the boat. Trinidad would sail it back to Jamaica, but not to Kingston, but rather to the other side of the island, where it would be completely retrofitted and given a new commission. Lester's uncle, the banker, had already expressed an interest in purchasing it. He would help Lester with the assets, be an emissary to the Jamaican government and police, and make sure everyone would be happy and prosper from this new-found wealth. They would likely form a new educational corporation, which would help support the new school Lester was planning on opening. They would likely help with some of the crumbling infrastructure around the school, such as roads, sewers and other necessities, but that was for later.

Finally, it was time for Bill and his crew to say goodbye. So far, they had not been given any money or treasure, but Bill wasn't worried. They all stood on the beach together. Everyone hugged and spoke about how they would all meetup in a few months in Jamaica. Lester had already sent feelers out to the government about setting up a new school in the country for wayward boys and girls to help set them on the right path. And, since he would be self-funded and did not need government money, they were all too pleased to streamline his charter through, after a few incidentals had been taken care of, of course.

Lester formally shook Bill's hand. I owe you a debt, Captain Bill, which I may never be able to repay, but in the meantime...," He gestured and two of his men carried one of the treasure chests up the gangplank of the PT boat and set it on the deck. "For now, this will have to do."

Thank you Captain," Bill said. I am looking forward to a nice vacation in Jamaica!"

They both stepped back in the sand and saluted each other. Bill and his crew returned to the PT boat. Manolo and Miguel pushed it off away from the shore and jumped aboard as Bill fired up the engines. They slowly backed back up the channel until they were in the open sea. Bill turned the boat around and pushed the throttle forward heading toward the coast. Jack, John and Kimmi had a plane to catch back to California.

Once they were underway, Bill called Manolo and Miguel to the bridge. "Why don't we open that chest and see what they gave us?

Manolo and Miguel, both nodded and went over to open the chest. The lock sprung immediately. Bill throttled the boat down and John, Jack and Kimmi, also gathered around. Bill was looking over his shoulder at them as the boat slowed, and he lashed down the wheel to get a better look at what was inside.

There was a note on top, written on parchment paper laying on top of a heavy red cloth covering the contents. John picked it up and began to read,

"For my dear friends. Your curse is lifted. You could have kept all of this to yourself and never found us. But you did not. You did the right thing and have served us and the people of Jamaica. We are your lifelong friends and look forward to seeing you on our island. Bless you,
Captain Lester Smith"

"That was nice", said Bill.

"Yes," said John. No accent in his writing!" They all laughed. John looked up at Bill, "With your permission, Captain."

Bill nodded, "Go ahead then."

John set the note on the deck and removed the covering. They were shocked at what they saw inside. Stacks of solid gold bars, weighing one pound each, and there looked to be over two hundred of them. John whistled in amazement. There were also gold coins, Spanish medallions, solid gold crosses, chains and some daggers with rare and precious jewels.

Bill said, "Wow, he wasn't kidding! How much is this all worth?" he asked John.

"Well, the bricks alone are worth at least five million, not to mention the coins, medallions, the gold trinkets, daggers. I've gotta' believe, there is well over ten million here!"

Kimmi, Manolo and Miguel were jumping up and down clapping. Jack and John were giving each high fives and shouting with joy.

Only Bill was a little more sober about it. He said, "Hey guys, not to be a party pooper, but let's not count our chickens before they're hatched. We will need to make plans on how to best handle this. But the good news is, we have the treasure and we will need figure out what to sell, what to keep and see if John needs to do research on the precious artifacts. Actually, I am amazed Lester was so generous! Usually pirates are not like that at all!"

Kimmi spoke up, "He's not a pirate, he's a school teacher!" They all laughed.

Bill said to Manolo and Miguel, "Take the treasure below. You may have to make a few trips. Put it in my cabin and later we can all check it out, while we have a late supper tonight!"

An hour later, Kimmi came up to Manolo, who was standing next to Bill on the bridge. "Hey Manolo, I'm kind of hungry. Is there anything to eat?

Manolo looked up at Bill, who smiled knowingly, and nodded his head. Kimmi and Manolo went below to the small galley, which was deserted. "What would you like to…" was all Manolo could get out, before Kimmi, sobbing, threw her arms around his neck and kissed him on the lips. Manolo moved her to the bench seat and held her until her sobs became small hitches. "I'm so tired of saying goodbye, Manolo. I just want to be with you."

Manolo pushed her hands down and kissed her gently on the cheek. "Only a couple of months, Kimmi. Only a few short weeks and we can move to Jamaica and help them set up their school. You and your dad can catalogue the treasure, help with the school and *Capitain* Lester told me I could work there as well! Then we can all be together for at least a year. After that, we may be together for a lot longer!"

Kimmi pushed back and looked him in the eye, "Wait was that a proposal?" she asked.

Manolo shook his head, "When I propose to you, I will do it right, not in the galley of a PT boat! But you are not going anywhere, as far as I am concerned!"

Kimmi kissed him and they hugged each other for a long time. "Thank you, Manolo," She said, "I love you!"

THE END

EPILOGUE

SIX MONTHS LATER, BILL TREESE, MANOLO and Miguel pulled up to the dock at Kingston Harbor in the PT boat. They were met by the local Harbor Police and also the local police. The Harbor Police asked them to secure their weapons and would help them sail to a covered slip, where their boat would be locked away for the duration of their stay. They also had the Border Patrol present and Customs would be there soon to stamp their passports and to get them to the spot where they would be picked up. For the most part, all of the officials were extremely courteous and friendly.

The Harbor Police and the Boarder Patrol were fascinated by Bill's PT boat and wanted to know all about it. Bill gave them all a tour and then told them the history of PT boats in World War II, while they waited for the Customs officials to arrive. He told them the variations on the boats, how the Americans built three different models from competing companies, but that his Elco style boat was the fastest and most sea-worthy. He told them the boats were active in both the Pacific Theater, against the Japanese and also in the Atlantic against the Germans and the Italians. He told them about the role the PTs played on D-Day, in June 1944, during the Battle of Normandy in France, when the U.S. attacked at Normandy Beach. They joked with Bill that he was free to get drunk and beak a few laws so they could confiscate it for their own use! Bill laughed good naturedly and offered to take them all out for a spin before they left the island. "You will enjoy the speed, but the ride is a little rough," he told them. After that, more officials arrived and they were properly processed into the country. Even the Customs officials, notoriously stiff and formal, seemed to relax around Bill and his crew.

They were taken by a taxi to a small bar and grill in Kingston, where they got out and went inside.

Suddenly, Manolo looking around spotted Jack sitting there with a lady. "Jack!" yelled Manolo, "You are here!"

They all went over and hugged each other. Jack said, "This is my bride, Lisa, we've been married a long time, but she is still my bride!"

Lisa put out her hand to Manolo and Miguel and they shook it warmly. To Bill she turned and hugged him tightly, "You old salt!" she kissed him on the cheek, "Thank you for saving my Jack's life a million times!"

Bill smiled and hugged her tight, "Yes, Lisa, it's nice to meet the pretty face behind the good doctor!" They both laughed.

They all sat down. They had about an hour before they were going to be picked up.

Bill asked, "So how's the food here in this place?"

Jack shrugged, "Beats me. We just got here." They looked over the menu, but it was kind of confusing. It was half in English and half in local Jamaican dialect. Jack continued, "I understand the jerk chicken, but what is ackee and saltfish? Or escoveitch fish? Or callaloo?" Jack looked confused.

The waitress came over to take their order. She was a young and very pretty local girl, dressed in a short pantsuit, with a tight white apron and tee-shirt on, which said:

Everyone on my island is a beautiful part of my family!

"What would you like?" she asked.

Jack spoke up, "We accept defeat." He looked at her name tag. It said ***Amancia.*** "Your name is pretty. What does it mean?"

She smiled, "It is Jamaican and it means someone who loves unconditionally."

Jack smiled, "Is it true?" he asked earnestly.

"Yes. My whole life, I have always loved without conditions or borders and without exception."

Jack looked her in her eyes, "I have no doubt about that. I love your tee-shirt, by the way! What would you recommend we order? We're kind of lost."

She smiled, showing even white teeth. "I've got you," she said. She collected all of their menus and, flashing a grin, she spun around and returned to the kitchen.

In a few minutes, she reappeared with another server, carrying their food on several plates. There was an excellent cheese nachos dip with fish, beans and vegetables, pulled pork sliders with pineapple, a large fish dish to share, a plate of local fruit and five Red Stripe beers. Without hesitation, they all dug in and ate everything.

She came back a couple of times to check on them, but they were still eating without saying anything. She smiled and, after it looked like they were done, she brought over some sweet potato pudding for dessert. "What is this?" Jack asked.

Amancia smiled. "It is the specialty of the house, sweet potato pudding. It is a local delicacy here and is like nothing you have ever tasted. We call it hell a top, hell a bottom and hallelujah in the middle!" She cut up several pieces and served it to them. There was a sweet custard layer on top and on the bottom, but with soft, tasty pudding in the middle. It was incredible.

After lunch, Amancia came back and, looking at all the empty plates asked, "How was it?" She smiled at them.

"Perfect!" they all said. She continued, "Are you here as tourists? Or do you have somewhere to go?"

Bill spoke up, "We are seeing a very good friend of ours, who just started a school in the country not too far from here!"

Amancia beamed, "You mean Captain Lester Smith and his new school! My brother goes there! He was headed for a bad seed, but my parents enrolled him! It didn't take long for Captain Lester to straighten him out! A big pirate like that can set anyone on the right path, ya!"

She went back and brought their tab, which Jack paid over Bill's protest. Jack added a very generous tip, suddenly realizing Amancia had comped them their dessert. He turned and thanked Amancia, assuring her they appreciated it, but it was not necessary.

Amancia smiled and said, "Please give my love and many thanks to Captain Lester! He has helped my family more than he would ever know.

THE LOST TREASURE OF THE JAMAICAN PIRATE

They all thanked her again and they went outside to be picked up.

The small bus arrived about five minutes later. It was driven by one of Lester's crew they recognized from the boat. It was Reggie.

"Hello, my friends! " he cried as they got on the bus. "Welcome to I and I island. Good flight and sea trip I hope!"

Bill spoke up, "Yes, Reggie, no problems, even with Customs."

"You can thank Lester for that one, ya! The local police and government officials have become our best friends!"

Jack said, "Reggie, this is my wife, Lisa." Lisa put out her hand and Reggie shook it, "It's nice to meet you," she said.

Reggie smiled, "Likewise, Miss!"

Lisa asked, "How far is it?"

"About an hour, depending on if we run into someone herding sheep and blocking the road. Then two hours!" They all laughed.

The ride was bumpy, over a dirt road part of the way and a paved road the rest of the way. After a little over an hour, they pulled up to the school. The banner out front said in large letters:

CAPTAIN LESTER SMITH'S SCHOOL FOR OUR LITTLE BROTHERS AND SISTERS.

"Cute name," said Bill. Jack jumped up and said, "Let's get off! I can't wait to see this!"

Reggie opened the door of the bus and everyone disembarked.

They all began to walk around the grammar school compound with Reggie. Suddenly, they spotted Kimmi walking toward them. She ran to them with outstretched hands, "Hi guys, I'm so happy you're here!" One by one, she hugged Bill, Jack, Lisa and Miguel, but she saved her best hug for Manolo! They all laughed as she jumped up in his arms, hugging and kissing him full on the lips. She looked into his eyes, "I missed you so much!" she added.

"Where is your dad?" asked Bill.

"He's in the Archive Room, working on the artifacts. He said to find him when you guys got here!"

"Come on," said Reggie, "Trinidad is around here somewhere.

They finally found Trinidad in the main office, who got up and gave them hugs all around! "It is so good to see our friends again!" Trinidad said, as he hugged them all again. "Let's go look around Captain Lester's school. I think you will all be very impressed with what we have done so far!"

Trinidad showed them the classrooms, the church, which was Christian, but non-denominational, the gym, the library, the music department, the drama department, the dance studio, the cricket field, the rugby field and a large cafeteria, where they could still smell the delicious leftovers from lunch. The campus was large and spread out, but still felt comfortable and intimate, because everyone walking around wore big smiles on their faces and there was much laughter. Adults, teenagers and children mingled and walked around freely.

"Where is Lester?" Bill asked.

Reggie said, pointing, "There he is at the basketball courts, on his knees, playing with the fourth graders!"

They looked out but did not recognize Captain Lester. Bill

spoke up, "Where is he?"

Trinidad smiled and yelled out, "Lester, our friends are here to see you, *mon!*"

Lester stopped, even as he let the last eight-year-old score above his head. "Whoa, you got me again, little *mon!*" he said.

The eight-year-old squealed with delight and jumped up in the air. He ran back to his teammates, high-fiving all of them, with a huge smile on his face!

Lester stood up and walked up to them. Captain Lester Smith had changed. He was clean-shaven and his hair was cut short. He looked more like a businessman than a pirate. He was very handsome and walked up to them with an air of authority.

"Hello, my maties!" he said. They were all dumbstruck at his change in appearance. Kimmi, who had been shocked a few months ago at his change in appearance, was the first to speak, "Isn't Captain Lester really handsome!" she blurted out.

They all laughed. Manolo put his arm around her and said good naturedly, "Hey, Kimmi, maybe we should head back to the boat, or maybe the U.S.A., or maybe Mars! What do you think, Kimmi?"

Lester smiled and strode up to Kimmi, He embraced her loosely. "Thank you, girl, but I think you only have your eyes for one *mon*, ya!"

Kimmi smiled and looked up at Lester, "Yes sir!" she said, "Is that an order from the headmaster, sir?"

"Absolutely, girl! Be smart. Good ones, boys and girls, only come around once in a while, ya!"

Bill Treese looked around, "Well, Lester, it looks like you have pulled it off. Nice school, nice kids. I even noticed a church chapel. Are you performing marriages as well?"

Lester smiled, "Ya, *mon,* I am an ordained minister. We do weddings, baptisms, funerals and Sunday services. Are you surprised?"

Bill smiled. "No, not a lick. I had no question you would become a great man, given the right circumstances. And you have become that man. I am happy for you and excited for your future!"

"Thank you, Bill," Lester said. "So then did you look around? See our school. See our babies we will turn into good men and women? No one will harm them here. No one will persuade them to be druggies and bad people. If so, they will have to deal with me!" He held up a fist. "I am still Lester Smith! And I will deal with anyone who tries to hurt my babies! They all know this and so do the parents!"

Bill nodded, "Fear in a good way!"

Lester smiled, "Ya *mon!*"

By then, John had come out, after being summoned by Reggie. He ran up and embraced them all. "I'm so happy you have all made it here!" John said. "We are making real progress and Captain Lester has played a huge part in helping us solve some of the mysteries of what we have found!"

Bill spoke up again, "Yes, I believe that and," speaking to Lester, "what of the treasure, my friend?"

Lester smiled, "Much of it is in my compound at my home, buried and behind fire-proof safes, locked away from the world, where it will stay. Maybe for a long time, ya. Some of the masterpieces are being looked over by John here," he nodded to Professor Waales, who had been working with the archaeologists of the island for the past six months. John also nodded, and said that he had been working with the local historical people. "Also," added Lester, "we have been donating monies to the local government and police in a way, of good faith, which will ensure our success. It seems to make them happy." He smiled, "So it is all good, *mon!*"

Bill nodded, "And what of your school? Is it good too? Will it be here to stay and do positive things for the people? Will it be a strong, positive stroke to the lives of these people who will place their trust in you?"

Lester smiled, "Even now, I and I are making it all happen. We have done more than the school, ya. We have invested millions, *mon*, into renovating our schools. We have installed water-filtration systems, built up the sewer system, added computer stations, refurbished our library, made our electricity and water safe for our children. There will be love. There will be peace. There will be education and our world will be a better place!"

Lester looked over at Jack. "We received your cases of books you wrote on chiropractic care. Also, your novels of adventure and romance. We have distributed them to the libraries on our island, and have several copies here on campus. Maybe some of the little ones will become chiropractors! What think ye, Jack? A worthy return for your donation of books?"

Jack smiled, "'Tis a worthy endeavor to create future chiropractors to serve Jamaica and the rest of the world, Captain Lester. Thank you!"

"Hey," said Lester to Trinidad, "What is the day, *mon?*"

"Friday," said Trinidad.

"Cool, *mon!*" said Lester, who looked at his watch. It was

about two o'clock, their time, now.

Lester happily said, "Watch this, *mon!*"

Suddenly, all of the classrooms opened up and the children from first to eighth grade came out. They lined up in rows and stood on the grounds. Then, over the speakers, came a recording by the children singing the sweet sounds of the old Jamaican folk song, *Day Oh.* All the children sang along with gusto and every fiber of their beings. They sang the entire song, even as their parents arrived by car, foot and bus, to collect their children from this most happy place!

Finally, they were done, as Lester, dropping to his knees, smiled happily, and as the children all lined past him, gave him a high-five, most having to jump in the air to reach him, then Trinidad and the rest of their men, before going home with their mommies and daddies.

Once they were done, Lester turned to them and said, "What think ye of me school, boys?"

They all responded by jumping up and hugging Lester, Trinidad and the rest of the school teachers. They were all overwhelmed by joy and happiness!

Bill, Jack, Lisa, John, Kimmi, Manolo and Miguel were all overcome with emotion!

The magic was just beginning!